In the
Shadow
of King's

In the Shadow of Kings
My Sister's Keeper
Bad Chemistry
Old Wounds

In the Shadow of King's

Nora Kelly

Poisoned Pen Press

Front Cover Photograph: Mary Bernard

Poisoned Pen Press
6962 E. First Ave. Ste 103
Scottsdale, AZ 85251
www.poisonedpenpress.com
sales@poisonedpenpress.com

Printed in the United States of America

The University and City of Cambridge exist, and so do King's College and the Chetwynd Room; but this is a work of fiction, not fact, and the characters and events described are entirely imaginary.

FOREWORD

When I wrote *In the Shadow of King's*, in the early eighties, Gillian Adams was a new character to me, someone I had to invent. In the beginning, I didnt even know her name. Since then, I've lived through three more books with her and have come to know her much better. Like a good friend, she has both changed and remained the same person. Gillian is older now, and she's solved several more murders on both sides of the Atlantic. *In the Shadow of King's* was her first case; lacking experience, she was more diffident than she later became. Her perspective, too, has altered with time, and she's had to make some hard decisions about her life.

What about Cambridge? Gillian was caught up in a murder investigation, but the place itself was the real mystery that fascinated her. Cambridge, too, has changed in fifteen years; it is richer now, and larger, and the traffic is worse. The university keeps building, and King's College Chapel charges an admission fee to tourists. But it is still possible to step from the crowded street through an archway into a silent, sun-drenched court, like a heroine in a fairytale who steps through a magic door from one world to another. It is still a place for the lucky few, still a place where tradition is worn like a crown and has the same weight. It is still seductive, and it still makes people angry. Gillian knows that as well as I do.

PROLOGUE

When Alistair Greenwood died that Monday afternoon, it was not from natural causes. Death came with a sudden violence that no one, least of all himself, expected. It must be said, however, that such a death had been—perhaps frequently—wished upon him.

He died in Cambridge, where he had lived; had he died there in his bed, the world would still have noticed the passing of Alistair Greenwood, professor of history, in the University of Cambridge. The manner of his death merely added a fillip of sensational vulgarity which he, had he been in a position to observe it, would have deplored.

Obituaries were written, and indeed read, not only in Cambridge, but in London, Paris and New York. Therein, in funeral majesty, were laid out his gifts, accomplishments and contributions: his unsurpassed erudition, his incisive scholarship, the elegant, powerful prose in which his diverse books were written. He had had few students, it was true, but wherever he pointed his divining rod platoons of scholars delved and invariably found water.

Alistair Greenwood was mourned. His death, it was agreed, was a calamitous loss to scholarship and civilization. And if, in some quarters, it gave cause for celebration, this was only a private matter.

CHAPTER 1

Gillian Adams had not seen Alistair Greenwood for fifteen years, yet, as it happened, she was there when he died. The day before, a warm Sunday in October, she took a train from London to Cambridge. In the afternoon, she was to have lunch at Professor Greenwood's house.

She had not been back to Cambridge since, doctorate in hand, she had ceased to be a student. She had returned to London many times; crossing the Atlantic was a habit. But something had always held her back from this little hour's journey on the train. Now, however, she was in London for a sabbatical year: she had no real excuse—no reason—for avoiding Cambridge, and she had been invited to give a lecture.

Gillian looked out of the window. The train from Liverpool Street was picking up speed as it left the outskirts of the city. She saw a dismal jumble of corrugated iron roofs and washing lines enclosed by a grimy brick wall. On the wall was painted a large message: WOG SLUM. The train ran on, past more walls and messages and into one of England's least interesting landscapes.

There were few passengers, and Gillian sat alone, suspended between two worlds. Cambridge was not just a town north of London; it was its own civilization, dense, polished, enclosed. Her friend Bee had offered to meet her at the station, but Gillian had asked her not to. She wanted to come back to Cambridge by herself, to be alone with her fading recollections before they were overlaid by the fresh colours of the present. Cambridge memories ought to come in shades of grey, she thought: grey windswept skies, grey stones, grimed by the centuries, mist shrouding the fields, rain. But memory did not choose grey; her images were all green and sunlit. The pinnacles of King's piercing the sky, golden light drenching courtyards and gardens, pale yellow hollyhocks and roses the colour of Jersey cream: these, and the emerald sweeps of lawn and meadow, were the colours of remembered Cambridge.

She mistrusted the selection process of her own mind. What was at work in the dust-laden recesses of memory, opening some boxes but leaving others undisturbed among the cobwebs? She could almost hear tissue paper crackling, as though the recollections that came to her now had been carefully packed, preserved from time's rust and rot. They seemed to her enchanting and useless, like outworn finery. She was not sure she wanted them any more, but they were her own: The Adams Collection. A pity that she couldn't have the whole lot auctioned at Sotheby's. There were plenty of people who would pay handsomely for a genuine set of Cambridge memories.

And how would it seem to her now, on this blue and gold October day? Would it be a small city in a flat green sea of fields: simply a piece of reality—changing, untidy, connected to the ordinary? Or would it be still separate and cocooned, a lingering dream? She felt reluctant and apprehensive, knowing that to return was to court a sense of loss.

The journey between one world and another is not necessarily a long one. The train slid past an unrewarding view of the university press buildings and pulled into the silent station. On Sunday morning, still quite early, nobody was about. Suddenly eager, she stepped on to the platform and walked through the station past the usual chalked notice of cancelled trains and out of the opposite door. She stood under an enormous sky, brushed here and there with attenuated, feathery clouds. Cambridge lay before her.

'Grantchester Meadows, please,' Gillian said to the taxi-driver. 'Number 51A.'

It took only a few minutes to drive through the southern edge of Cambridge to Bee's house in Newnham. Gillian peered out of the windows, looking for signs of change and seeing none. Doubtless they were there, but they were not of the dramatic sort she would notice. Station Road, Hills Road, Bateman Street, the Trumpington Road, and then across Coe Fen past a glimpse of the towers and gables of her own college rising up beyond a fringe of trees, and on to Grantchester Meadows, the little street that ran closest to the river in the south-western corner of Cambridge. This quarter of the city was called Newnham, and its outer edge, lying between the Barton Road and the Cam, was a pleasant neighbourhood, she remembered; dons lived there in large houses with pretty gardens. But its quiet streets did not mean much to her, although they lay just south of her college; they were part of the carapace that surrounded the centre where her memories lay.

She paid the driver, got out, and stood for a moment in front of Bee's house. It was not large, and the space in front of it could hardly be called a garden. It was a terrace house on the inner, not the river, side of the street; built of red brick, with two bay windows vertically stacked, it had a squat, cramped look. The white paint on the door-frame was blistered and peeling. She rang the bell and waited. Above the door, a semicircular pane of glass was veiled by a dispirited spiderweb, but the spider had decamped, leaving behind only the translucent exoskeletons of old victims.

Beatrix Hamilton opened the door, drink in hand. 'Hullo, Gillian. You've come just in time.'

Gillian stepped into the dim interior and barked her shin on a box of ill-assorted domestic items. 'Hullo, Bee. Just in time for what?'

'For the third act,' said Bee, slamming the door. 'I'm leaving the doll's house.'

Gillian could think of nothing to say; conventional regrets and brittle wit seemed equally inappropriate.

'But don't think you'll be in the way. After all, it's not the end of an era, it's just another divorce. And we need a demilitarized zone.'

'How's Toby?' Gillian asked, as it passed through her mind that Bee's house was unlikely to prove a comfortable retreat from the rest of Cambridge.

'When he gets over the irritation induced by any disturbance of his routine, he'll be relieved.'

'And you?'

'Fed up. Leave your suitcase by the stairs and come into the kitchen. Toby's gone off. In every sense. What do you want? Coffee? I don't suppose you want whisky; it isn't usually what I want on Sunday morning.' She led the way down the dark corridor to the kitchen. 'By the way, Herr Professor Alistair Greenwood expects us at one.'

It was just after ten o'clock. 'Coffee, please,' said Gillian. 'If it's a typical Sunday lunch, there will be oceans of drink. I don't want to disgrace myself in Greenwood's herbaceous borders.'

'How do you know he's got any?'

'He's bound to. Whoever heard of an English gentleman without a garden? I didn't know you were coming to lunch— I'm glad. Is Toby coming too?'

Bee was filling the kettle. The small kitchen was brighter than the corridor, but it had a stale, disused air. Dirty coffee cups and a variety of glasses crowded the counter next to the sink, and a jumble of empty milk bottles stood by the back door, but nothing in the room invited one to think of food, except perhaps the presence of a refrigerator. Gillian guessed that there would be ice in it, and something horrible and mouldy in the vegetable drawer. A table occupied one corner of the room; on it rested a cardboard box containing stacks of computer paper and a coffee-pot.

Bee found the coffee and retrieved the pot. 'Yes, we're both coming. A gesture of courtesy, I surmise, since we're putting you up. A fringe academic like me would never be invited, otherwise.' She glanced up from her search for the coffee filters, and her look was almost hostile. 'I may add, we're being terribly civilized about the divorce. No shouting, no smashed glass. Just a little knife play in the dark.'

The kettle reached a spitting boil and a scalding burst of steam pushed up the lid. 'Why has Alistair Greenwood invited me to lunch?' Gillian inquired.

'Noblesse oblige, my dear. Professor Greenwood is a public monument, and the public must be allowed in sometimes. Well, not the public public, but interested scholars.'

'How terribly flattering.'

'Indeed. But one goes. You wouldn't turn down an audience with the Pope, would you?'

'Not if I were promised a good lunch.'

Bee smiled a little. 'You'll certainly have that. But I shouldn't count on enjoying it.'

'I'm not. I'll probably be too nervous.'

Having at last assembled everything necessary to produce a potful of coffee, Bee dumped some hot water into the filter, rinsed two cups and set them on a battered tray decorated with a series of Victorian views of Cambridge. 'Or too angry. By the time you finish your third glass you'll want to bludgeon him with his own Burgundy bottle.'

'An alluring prospect. Why will I?'

'Most people do. Or so I hear, not ever having had the privilege of his august company. He's an arrogant bastard, as you must know. But maybe you'll like him. You always had a weakness for the silver tongue, as I recall.' She looked vaguely about. 'I'm sorry. There aren't any biscuits.'

'Never mind. I don't want any.'

'Good. I must pull myself together and do some shopping one of these days. Toby's been dining in college, and I've hardly been eating at all. He's moving into rooms there, and we'll rent the house.'

'Where will you live then?'

'Some grotty little pigeonhole further out. That's all I'll be able to afford. University drudges are notoriously underpaid.'

'What are you doing nowadays?'

Bee picked up the tray. 'The same old thing. Supervisions. I have about ten students. I see each of them for about an hour a week, or sometimes two, and they bring me their essays on *El Cid* and other monuments of Spanish lit. I keep my hand in. Somehow it's easier to go on with research if one has a formal connection to university life—even such a minor one. And it's necessary to earn one's keep.' She marched down the corridor in front of Gillian. Now that her eyes were more accustomed to the gloom, Gillian noticed that the corridor was made darker and narrower by bookshelves all along one side. At the far end, next to the front door, was the sitting-room. This too was rather dark, although it faced south. Frayed curtains were partly drawn across the bay window. The room was cold, untouched by the bright October morning, and smelled strongly of the books which lined three of the walls from floor to ceiling. It was a damp, papery, mouldering smell, not unpleasant, but impossible to ignore. The chill pressed upon them like the wintry air in a disused chapel, and Gillian had a sense of being entombed among the books as she envisaged the slow spread of brown spots through their leaves, the dust settling untouched on their spines.

'Will your pigeonhole have a library?'

'You may well ask. I don't know what I'll do with all these. I never look at them now, but I can't bear to part with them, or even to put them away. And I haven't even acquired very many in the last few years.' Bee put down the tray and sat with an air of exhaustion.

In the room were two immense and hideous armchairs, a moth-eaten Victorian sofa, a heavy old oak desk, a gilt clock, unwound, and a Georgian tilt-top table badly in need of polish. A threadbare Turkey carpet covered some of the floor. Bee got up and pushed back the curtains, and more light came in. The carpet, in shades of blue, glowed feebly back at the sky.

Gillian stepped over a paint flake as big as a butter plate. She looked up. Over her head drooped an enormous curl of thick paint. It sagged away from the ceiling, and where the paint had detached itself, cracked, stained plaster could be seen. Gillian sat down, shifting her chair away from the curl. It looked stable enough, even eternal. But there was a film of dust on the table, and the cold air was very still. Perhaps the loose paint, like the drawings at Lascaux, would be unable to withstand the acidic heat of humanity pressing into the room and would disintegrate as they sat there.

Bee passed Gillian a cup of coffee. 'So you've come back to Cambridge at last,' she said abruptly. 'How does it feel?'

'I don't know yet. I just got here. Edgy, I guess.'

'It won't be strange and new. It hasn't changed.'

'Oh, come on. Of course it has—women in men's colleges, no gowns—'

Bee shrugged. 'It doesn't feel different to me. Yes, there are women students. But the gentlemen up there in the stratosphere hardly take any notice. They don't need to. Cambridge is still elitist, closed, run by a bunch of old men living in some other century—like your friend Greenwood. And there may be female students in large numbers, but female fellows are about as common as female bishops. It's a men's club still.'

Gillian regarded her friend thoughtfully. It was many years since they had lived in Newnham College. Then, the bond between them had been, like the friendships of boarding-school, a compound of humour, domestic intimacy and common hardships, and it had seemed unbreakable. They had met each other at intervals after Gillian left Cambridge, and, relying only a little on the schoolgirl existence they had once shared, had easily found themselves again at no great distance from where they had left off. But now it had been three years since their last meeting, and a barrier stood between them. An astringent directness in Bee, which had once brought them together, had changed quality, had shrivelled and hardened. Life had been a burden of disappointments—how many was not yet clear—and her anger had become indiscriminate. Gillian smelled disaster in the air and was assailed by the conviction that it would have been wiser not to come to Cambridge at all. She searched for something to say. 'You should visit North America, Bee. Spend some time at a few non-elitist universities like mine. You would think more kindly of Cambridge.'

'I don't want to think more kindly of Cambridge. I'll leave that to you.'

Gillian drank her lukewarm coffee. 'I don't know what I think of it. It's been too long, and there's something unreal about it—either in my mind or in the place itself.'

'In both. In both. That's where the snare lies. You tell me what you think when you've been here for a few days.'

Gillian put down her cup. 'Why don't you leave Cambridge, then?' she asked directly.

'That's like asking a woman why she doesn't leave her husband.'

'But you *are* leaving your husband.'

'Believe me, it's easier.' Bee laughed without mirth. 'Listen. Being in Cambridge has been, for me, the definition of a life. Marriage could never be that. And as for Toby, he's hardly the man I did marry. His little academic talent has dried up on him, and he's taken refuge in all the pompous old rituals of exclusion that survive in his benighted institution. We don't see anything the same way any more. You're not married, I suppose?'

'No.' But she hadn't ruled it out. She thought of Edward, whom she hadn't seen in four days.

'Do you mind being alone?'

'No. I quite like it most of the time. And I haven't taken a vow of chastity.' She was finding the conversation difficult; their withered intimacy cast a shadow of expectation between them, each question, each answer, was exposed and bare, a rock upon which nothing grew.

'Are you seeing someone in London, then?'

'Yes.' Gillian made an effort. 'Edward Gisborne. He's a Scotland Yard detective.'

'You're joking.'

'I'm not. He's probably pursuing some miscreant through the sewers right now. He catches murderers, among other things.'

'Really? How convenient. We'll ring him up after Greenwood's lunch then, when we'll need him.' They both laughed. For a moment, Gillian glimpsed the old, acerbic but friendly Bee.

'What's he like?' Bee asked.

'Wonderful,' replied Gillian shortly. 'But perhaps impossible.'

Bee offered her the smile of a comrade in arms. 'I know the feeling.'

Then the door opened, and Toby Fox came in. Bee stiffened, and the light died out of her eyes.

Toby was breezy. 'Hullo, Gillian. Long time and all that. How are you?'

'Fine, thanks. And you?'

Toby was a physicist, but she had forgotten what sort. He was short and slight and attractive in a consumptive, poetical style accentuated by an intentional raffishness of dress and manner. His skin was pale, but his hair and eyes were dark, and his thick, straight eyebrows gave his face a serious look. His movements were quick, as was his speech, which ran with glittering opacity over rough surfaces like rapids in a stream. She had noted that years earlier, when she had first met him; it was a verbal style one encountered frequently in Cambridge. His clothes hadn't altered either: he was wearing battered brown trousers and a grey cardigan that was out at the elbows. In Gillian's view, this sartorial approach was somewhat depressing, but it was a distinct improvement over that of the American scientist, who tended to favour drip-dry shirts with plastic pen holders in the breast pocket, and, with mysterious frequency, trousers that were too short.

He reached two fingers into a pocket and twitched out a flattened cigarette and some matches. Lighting up absently, he dropped into a chair and answered Gillian without a glance at Bee. 'Oh, splendid. I'm about to join the jolly company of bachelors—rooms in college, wine, women, brilliant intellectual repartee every night. I'm an enviable fellow, wouldn't you say?'

'Would you rather be in a bed-sit off Mill Road?' Bee inquired acidly.

Toby ignored this. 'So, charming and successful Gillian, what are you doing on this crumbling isle?' Gillian looked covertly at Bee, whose face was closed like a coffin. The word successful had had a sting in it. Toby went on: 'After all, I was born here, you've got no such excuse. You, the historian of our halcyon days, why do you come poking around in the ruins? I should have thought we'd entered the province of the archaeologists by now. There's plenty for them to do, excavating past glories, while we sit like old men remembering the conquests of youth.'

'Historians no longer walk alone, Toby. We couple with archaeologists and all sorts of strange bedfellows. Besides, I have a taste for decay.'

'So do the English. But then we've had to develop a taste for it. We haven't got anything else left.'

'The predilection was there anyway. Think of the English notion of a formal occasion: dinner jackets that have turned green with age and wine that has turned brown.'

'Rather that than pink dinner jackets and Coca-Cola.'

'It is obvious that our social spheres have been widely different. I am glad to say that I have never seen a pink dinner jacket.'

'No, I suppose not. America simply can't be as awful as we wish it were.'

'No,' Gillian replied equably, 'it's not. But the northwest, in particular, does create an appreciation of the subtle virtues of decline. Everything there is so new. It feels flimsy and one-dimensional—makes one long for the rich odour of decay.'

'You've come to the right place, then. Decay we can provide in abundance. Any flavour you fancy.' Toby stubbed out his cigarette.

'What about Cambridge?' Gillian asked. 'It must be relatively untouched.'

'Untouched. Yes—that's exactly the problem,' said Bee.

Toby cut in. 'Do save it, Bee, until you two are alone. I simply can't face "Women in Cambridge" again. Especially on Sunday morning.' Bee raised her eyebrows at Gillian as if to say, 'See?' Toby went on talking. 'Of course we don't feel the pinch to the same extent as many other places, but it's unquestionably there, especially in the poorer colleges. We find ourselves obliged to make unpalatable choices. We can't hire additional fellows as we'd like to; my college needs another lawyer, for example. We have to find £100,000 to repair the organ, and the chapel needs a new roof, which will doubtless cost the same again. All the stonework wants cleaning. The list is endless. Until you've seen the Bursar's reports, you simply cannot imagine how expensive the upkeep of these old college buildings is. And there are other problems.'

'Why, yes,' Bee remarked. 'Times are hard. You were complaining just the other day that the wine at dinner was only a Rhône. Where are the Beaunes of yesteryear?'

'Precisely, my dear,' Toby drawled. 'We really must find a benefactor to endow the cellar, or God knows what we'll be drinking in twenty years' time.'

'So are the colleges doing a lot of fund-raising these days?' Gillian asked.

'I'm afraid we have to. But at least we don't yet select our Masters on the basis of their skill with the begging bowl, as I understand American universities do now.'

'Perhaps not. But you wouldn't turn down a great big vulgar American donation, would you?' snapped Gillian, her irritation getting the better of her.

'Of course not. The bigger and more vulgar, the better.' He turned the subject. 'What about London, Gillian? You lived there in the Sixties, didn't you? Don't you find it different now?'

'That's hard to say. I probably had a different perspective on it then. And one's soundings are so parochial, you know. A single well-remembered building is torn down and one is instantly certain that the whole city is being destroyed. But I suppose London feels more extreme these days—both the richness and the poverty are more conspicuous. It reminds me of New York, where everyone talks constantly about the problems, and how expensive it is, and the deterioration of everything...and yet life keeps going on all around at a fantastic pace, fecundity defying the mourners. I think London is a marvellous city.'

Toby was tenderly straightening a squashed cigarette. 'Mm. Well, London will always look better from the vantage-point of an American salary.'

'Don't complain,' said Bee. 'At least you have a real salary. You're not underemployed, like me.'

'You can thank Mrs. Thatcher's education cuts for that.'

'Nonsense. Thatcher hardly ripples the surface here. Cambridge is the reason. Cambridge—as it was in the beginning, is now, and ever bloody well shall be, so far as I can see.' Bee glared at them both.

'Amen,' responded Toby. 'What else should it be, my dear? And what's more, I hope that it remains sufficiently cushioned to be unrepentantly elitist in its choice of faculty *and* students. You can't have a good university without a restrictive admissions policy. They've tried that in America. That's the trouble with America: they try everything. Everyone, with the exception of those children of the left who never grow up, recognizes that any country—every organization of human beings—needs an elite to run it properly. This place is a factory which produces that kind of elite. If you destroy it, dilute its quality, the world will be the poorer. And what will you gain? Another Salford. The world has no need of more Salfords. If you believe that the intellect produces anything of value, then you have to believe in Cambridge: you must support the existence of places which give the best intellects the best opportunities. You must ensure that they prosper.'

'I'm not arguing about the existence of Cambridge. I'm objecting to its prejudices. I don't believe women should be excluded.'

'Hardly anybody does.'

'Oh, really? I'd say it's one of the commonest beliefs in Cambridge. It's just less acceptable to say it out loud now.'

'That's something, anyway,' Gillian put in.

Toby sighed. 'Oh, very well, ladies, "Women in Cambridge" it is. But really there's no need. Only three men's colleges are left, and there's a pitched battle being fought behind the walls at Pembroke.'

'Is that so?' inquired Gillian with interest. 'Anyone dead yet?'

'All of 'em,' said Bee, *sotto voce.*

Toby laughed tolerantly. 'I'm sure some of them hope to be before six centuries of scholarly monasticism are tossed into the dustbin. And why shouldn't a couple of men's colleges remain? There are two women's colleges. Besides, something like thirty-five per cent of the undergraduates are women now. That looks irreproachably egalitarian to me. More qualified female candidates can't be found at the moment. It would be mistaken from every point of view—including yours—to lower the entrance standards in order to admit more women. For that matter, the same goes for students from comprehensives. The best we can do is admit as many as we can who are able to meet our requirements. Otherwise we'll be cheating them—and ourselves.'

'Save the speeches,' Bee said tiredly. 'Women students aren't the front line this decade. What about women on the faculty? What about fellows? Lecturers? Where are they?'

'I can see the dust of their marching feet on the horizon, my dear. Doubtless the place will be overrun with intellectual amazons at about the same time the wine runs out.'

'Oh, what's the point?' Bee muttered.

'My sentiments precisely. I shall retreat and leave the field of honour to you.' He got up and moved towards the door.

Bee put down her half-empty cup. 'I'll go and change.'

'Into Dr. Jekyll, I hope,' said Toby, firing a Parthian shot from the hall. Bee got up and brushed past him without deigning to reply. Gillian sat dolefully in her chair, while Toby hovered in the hall near the door, fiddling with a match. It would not light. 'Damn!' he said fretfully, trying another. It sputtered, flared and went out. 'I'll have to find some more. I don't know why I bother to smoke these things; they're so healthy they taste of nothing. I'd better dress, I suppose.' He gazed about, as if expecting a set of clothes to materialize. Then he wandered off, tossing a final remark over his shoulder. 'You must be looking forward to your lecture tomorrow, Gillian: your chance to enter the arena fully armed.'

Alone in the chilly room, Gillian thought to herself that he couldn't always have been so poisonous, or presumably Bee would never have married him. What had done it? Was it just the soured marriage? She sat still, listening for the sound of mould growing. A flat film of smoke drifted and swirled slowly in the light from the window. Then a faint creak above her head made her look up at the curl of paint, which was swaying ever so slightly and seemed to droop a little more. Gathering up the cold cups, she carried them down the dark corridor to the kitchen and went hesitantly upstairs to find her room.

CHAPTER 2

Gillian remained upstairs for some time, prolonging the simple tasks of unpacking and changing her clothes. Arraying herself in white linen, as if she were soon to step into a tumbrel, she thought about Alistair Greenwood. Fifteen years before, she had been a history student and he a Cambridge historian of increasing renown, who at the age of thirty-five had exuded a celestial unapproachability rarely equalled even among those who had had another decade or two to perfect it. She did not expect him to remember her. The Cambridge Historical Society had asked her to come and lecture, and the invitation to lunch was a courteous prelude, that was all. She was conscious of a cowardly impulse to excuse herself, but it was impossible not to go. Moreover, she was curious. Interested, she had to confess, was too elevated a description for her attitude. She wanted to know what the famous Alistair Greenwood was really like.

For famous he had become: a professor, occupant of the Regius Chair, a great man of European intellectual history. The adjective 'eminent' had so often been coupled with his name that Gillian had taken to thinking of him as His Eminence, Professor Greenwood, and picturing him in scarlet robes. His name resounded in university classrooms and could be heard in the din of argument; it appeared in *The Times* when he wrote a book, or when the heat of some intellectual fray attracted public attention. He was frequently interviewed and detonated his opinions like firecrackers at a staid tea-party. The books he wrote, if few and spare, were works not only of history, but of literature, in which the past moved, breathed, appeared whole. His arguments had the clarity of utter self-assurance. His best-known work, *Ruling Ideas: The Transformation of European Thought in the Eighteenth Century*, was like a Cellini: small, but so elegant, rich and perfected that the mere idea of a larger work was rendered grotesque. Copies could be found in every university library and on nearly every history student's bookshelf. Even rather uninspired bookshops frequently kept it in stock, she could not help noticing. Alistair Greenwood, she reflected with the envy felt by those whose royalties do not pay the bills, must be living well off the proceeds of scholarship.

All in all, he was an extraordinary specimen, and she wanted a closer look at him. Even at a distance, he was not a man one would forget, and she remembered perfectly how he had looked fifteen years earlier. Tall, lean, fair-haired and tweedy, he was an instantly recognizable English product. His head was narrow and elongated, with a high forehead, and his skin, pale, almost translucent, was stretched tightly over the bones, barely softening their fine angularity. He had a strong knife-ridge of a nose, beautifully carved ears, and a thin, hard mouth. 'Frightfully attractive, if you don't object to a whiff of the monastery,' one of Gillian's fellow students had said, which was approximately correct. He was undoubtedly handsome, but he inspired no physical response; some element was missing. Intimacy, Gillian supposed. One could not imagine it in any form.

He had taken no notice of Gillian when she was a student, so far as she knew. He rarely noticed students at all, and his chosen few were, without exception, male. Gillian had often heard him lecture, however. Then he was performer for a hushed throng; he held his audience rapt, convinced, as the vast, messy, intractable agglomeration of evidence that is the raw material of history was sorted with wondrous efficiency into a self-evident pattern. His assurance enveloped the students, lifted them out of the mire of facts. He seemed to be poised effortlessly above his terrain, elevated by the broad wingspan of his knowledge, aware of the large shapes of mountains and rivers, yet able to swoop upon a mere mouse moving in the stubble far below.

Some of his foes castigated these lectures as an intellectually dubious form of theatre, a sort of conjuror's trick by which the sheer force of personality and language overwhelmed the argument itself. Their ears missed the reassuring sound of academic wheels creaking. To Gillian, who after one of his best lectures had come blinking into the grey light out of doors and walked straight into a post, it was as if he had found the philosopher's stone. He turned the common matter of history into art. And it was, in part, this alchemy, this unrepeatable, mysterious creation of gold, which ultimately divided opinion about him. His works were held up as masterpieces or dismissed as mirages. His gifts did not inspire moderate views.

Whatever Greenwood's detractors said, they could not accuse him of shunning contradiction. He welcomed it, turning out each challenge like an untidy drawer in order to retain any small items of value before consigning most of the contents to the rubbish heap. He was virtually unassailable in argument, armoured with his own arrogant mastery. Gillian had seen him attacked, had seen him rend his opponents with cold pleasure. He referred with graceful deference to the fine work of other historians, but he seemed sublimely unaccustomed to modifying his opinions. And friends? She didn't know whether he had any. So far as she had been able to determine from her outpost among the history students, he had had no intimates in the history faculty, only acolytes and enemies. Now that he was a great man, he was doubtless as invulnerable as ever, and more solitary.

She looked at her watch. In less than an hour she would be sitting down to lunch. She could not imagine the conversation, that is, her part in it, and devoutly hoped that Greenwood was in the habit of lecturing his guests as well as his students. Pushing her anxiety from her, she began to compose a list of the places she most wished to see again: Newnham (her own college), Queens', Clare, Trinity and King's. She slipped into a reverie, thinking of Trinity, its dark, forbidding gateway and, hidden behind, the serene geometry of its vast courts. The vision lingered; then it was superseded by the primal image: the high, narrow immensity of King's College Chapel. Massive, yet poised as delicately as the arch of the sky, that branching roof in cool and lofty silence seemed to hover over all of Cambridge.

Eventually, Gillian descended the stairs again and found Toby and Bee in the kitchen. They had dressed and applied a social varnish to their manners; the atmosphere was one of a guarded cease-fire. Toby was wearing an old blazer and a soft white shirt; he looked respectable in the negligent way that was usual in Cambridge. Bee, in a scarlet cotton sundress, her dark hair brushed back and her mouth painted, looked more like the Bee that Gillian remembered: the big, strong, aggressively sexy woman who had cut an easy swathe through Cambridge's pale young men. Bee had once said that she was built like a draught animal but did not mean to be treated like one. She had muscular legs, wide shoulders, and a lean body with no frivolous protrusions. Her face was large and bony, with dramatic planes and angles, the eyes set wide apart, the mouth generous. Gillian had seen, long ago, some splendidly theatrical photographs of her; she had looked spectacular in Sassoon's famous angular cut. But then she had looked quite splendid even before she was fully awake in the morning, reminding Gillian of Gerda, the beautiful giantess of Norse myth. Now, at the end of her thirties, she was not so impervious to the ravages of mood and time or the effects of dress; she had looked hagridden earlier that day, pale, dry-skinned, her dark horsey hair hanging stiffly about her face, strain showing at the mouth and eyes. Her body had seemed smaller inside her clothes, which had been creased and mottled with fuzz, as though she had wrapped herself in an old blanket and slept for a few restless hours on the sofa.

Bee poured a whisky and drank it while Gillian and Toby chatted inconsequentially about Channel crossings and travelling in France. Then it was time to go. The old red Mini was parked on the street in front of the house; Bee had the keys and got into the driver's seat. It crossed Gillian's mind that perhaps Bee should not be driving, but risking death being marginally preferable to having another row, she said nothing. Possibly Toby had arrived at a similar conclusion, since after a perceptible hesitation he climbed into the back. Gillian slid into the seat next to Bee and tried to close the door.

'Slam it,' said Bee, starting the engine. 'It's like everything else around here: no response unless you use violence.' Gillian banged the door shut and groped for a seat-belt as Bee revved the engine brutally. 'One day, Toby will start the car and the body will simply disintegrate around him into a pathetic little heap of rubble.'

'Are you going to put a bomb under the bonnet?' Toby inquired.

'I won't need to. Nature has her own slow-motion bomb called rust. That's oxidation to you high-powered Cambridge scientists. This car is merely an ambulatory coat of paint.' She performed a tidy U-turn and roared up the street. 'It's not far to Greenwood's house, Gillian. Little Camford is only about ten minutes out of Cambridge, towards London.'

They left Newnham and drove south on the Trumpington Road. The sun was bright on the tall trees, their leaves still barely touched with autumn colour.

'You must be looking forward to seeing your old haunts,' Toby remarked.

'Yes. I must say, I never took much notice of your part of Newnham when I was a student.'

'Why would you? It's not a centre of riotous student life, and the pubs are dreary.'

'My student life was not riotous,' Gillian said with dignity. 'I got that out of my system at boarding-school.'

'American boarding-schools must be different.' Toby opened the window and lit a cigarette. The prosperous outskirts of Cambridge had given way to flat fields. 'We didn't have the opportunity. Or perhaps it was just bad timing. I wish I'd been at school during the rebel years—refusing chapel and all that. It would have been more fun.'

'We didn't have chapel, I am relieved to inform you,' Gillian said.

'How maddeningly progressive. What did you have to rebel against?'

'Authority, of course. The form it took wasn't necessarily relevant. There were rules, so we broke them—but it didn't amount to much. I remember a feeble little riot we had once. There wasn't an issue; it was mere anarchy let loose upon the school.'

'What happened?'

'Nothing. Nothing at all. There was a mob. Everyone tore around in the middle of the night hoping something dreadful would happen by spontaneous combustion. Somebody played the drums—bongos, of course—and there was a bonfire. I forget what we burnt. Not books, at any rate. It was an entirely harmless affair, but the faculty were gratifyingly upset.'

'Was it fun?' Bee asked.

'Sort of. It relieved the monotony. But it was stupid. I remember feeling embarrassed, but not embarrassed enough to go to bed—in case I missed something.'

'Hardly another Watts, I take it.'

'Hardly. Just a portent of the Sixties. I was reminded of it once, years later in Vancouver, when a pack of students invaded that vicious bastion of privilege, the faculty club.

They sat around for a while, eating the bar snacks, while some of the faculty made agitated appeals and others wallowed in the excitement, hoping their ears heard the clarion call of revolution. Then they all went home. Now that was really embarrassing. Youthful insurrection was supposed to have some answers then. A student riot here would have about as much point, I suppose, but those days have gone.'

'I wouldn't mind a women's riot,' said Bee. 'The men had their turn in eighteen-ninety-seven when they rioted and hung an effigy of a woman in order to protest the admission of women for degrees. That was certainly an effective political action—women weren't admitted for degrees for another fifty years. Fifty years! Can you believe it? Not until our lifetime, Gillian.'

Gillian nodded. 'I know. And I distinctly recall remnants of that attitude here, even in the Sixties.'

'So do I,' said Bee with fervour. 'And I still see them now. All those old port-swillers, sitting around after dinner, secure in their self-importance just because they're here. Why should they change? By the time they die off, the younger men will be just like them. Look at Toby.'

Gillian refrained from doing so. She said slowly, 'But, you know, that didn't poison my time here. I suppose I wasn't aware enough, or just found it bizarre, like the initiation rites of some exotic tribe. It was part of the encrustation of tradition—like high table or the rule that only fellows can walk on the lawns.'

'It isn't your country,' Bee pointed out. 'And anyhow, those traditions aren't in the same category.'

'No. I suppose I would have found the same thing at Harvard much more shocking.' Gillian looked out at the blue sky. 'But I did take Cambridge seriously. My God, I was dazzled. I was so amazed to be here at all; I felt blessed, I wandered around breathing rarefied air. Cambridge was so beautiful, so ancient, so silent. It is the silence, that golden, cloistered silence in the courts that I remember best. It had the weight of eternity in it.'

'Silence,' Toby drawled. 'You must have done your wandering at odd hours. I never seem to get a moment's peace at college.'

'Try for a little realism, Toby,' Bee said over her shoulder. 'Your idea of a moment's peace is six uninterrupted hours.'

'Six hours isn't much to ask of eternity. Don't miss your turn.'

'I will not, thank you.'

Gillian fell silent, comparing her memories with this peculiar, cramped present. She had seen Cambridge through a gilded haze, but she had not been blind. She had thought: here are beauty, serenity, and greatness, here abides civilization. Would it now seem ossified and shrunken like her friends, a society turned stale and torpid and ingrown?

They passed through a village, and Bee turned abruptly off the main road. Two minutes later, they arrived at Little Camford. It was a small village. Gillian could see a handful of whitewashed cottages, their walls bulging gently, their thatched roofs somewhat seedy beneath wire netting. Beyond them were several larger houses of Victorian brick, set further back from the road, and a couple of small, new, stolid houses like bunkers. Next came a tiny, plain church with a square tower, half concealed amid sheltering trees. There was a graveyard beside it: smooth turf, a few worn and leaning stones. Dappled light fell on them through the leaves. Gillian thought how nice it would be to get out of the car. The dead looked like peaceful company.

Bee drove over a narrow bridge. Below it, the river sprawled on a stony bed, its dark surface flecked with a few yellow leaves. Two boys were fishing from the bank; ducks swam by, undisturbed. Beyond the bridge were one or two more houses and the pub. The latter was a compact building, high-roofed above a frenzy of half-timbering. It was as tidy as a ship, and the gravelled sideyard was filled with expensive cars in tasteful greys.

'They do very good food there,' Bee remarked super-fluously.

'Here we are, Gillian,' Toby said from the back. Beyond the pub lay a belt of trees, then a high brick wall began; it ran along the road for perhaps five hundred feet. Bee slowed and turned into a narrow leafy lane flanked on the right by a continuation of the same wall and on the left by a thick screen of trees and bushes through which Gillian could just see a stretch of empty field. The lane curved slightly, until the road behind was lost to view. Then it widened before a large entrance, where tall, green-painted gates stood open. Past these gates, the lane followed the wall until both curved out of sight again. Bee went through the gates and up a gravelled drive. 'Camford House,' she announced. The drive turned back almost parallel to the lane, passing through a small wood before turning again to approach a large, converted stable behind the house.

They stopped. Gillian got out of the car and stood beside it, taking the house in. She was to one side of it; as she had seen coming up the drive, the house faced east, towards the lane. It was a tall, austere structure of seventeenth-century brick, coloured a deep, rich, melancholy red, the hue of wine that is beginning to fade. Above the brick, and the rows of large sash windows trimmed in white, rose a steep-pitched, dormered tile roof, surmounted at either end by a stalwart chimney. It was a large, plain, unadorned, faultless house.

Gillian drew breath. 'How lovely to live in a house like that. One would enjoy a sense of perfection about one part of life, at least.'

'There's more,' said Toby from behind her. 'You'll see it when we go round to the other side. The back part is older, Elizabethan, I believe.'

Bee walked ahead of them along a gravelled path that led from the drive to the main entrance of the house. Her red dress flamed against the lawn like a poppy. Gillian began to follow, then she felt a hand on her shoulder. 'You ought to come back to Cambridge, Gillian. You would be at home here,' Toby said.

'Would I?' She turned her head to look at him and assess the intent of this remark. His hand stayed on her shoulder, so she moved away, not fancying the prospect of his sidling, crablike advances.

At that moment, the heavy front door of the house opened, and a figure, unmistakably that of Alistair Greenwood, emerged. Gillian had a long moment in which to observe him as he approached. He was more hawk-visaged than ever, the bones sharper, the eyes colder, the hair still thick but silvered over, the skin taut. His face could never have been described as fleshy; now it was a bare covering of the skull. He was lean and vigorous and predatory, only a slight thickening at the waist betraying the years of high table dinners.

'He looks terrifying,' Gillian muttered to Toby.

'That's because he is terrifying,' Toby muttered back. Then they were too close to say more.

Introductions were made, the conventional words uttered. They strolled round the corner of the house to the rose-garden, where chairs and tables had been set out.

'I'm delighted you could come; Cambridge is fortunate to have secured such an attractive guest,' was Greenwood's first remark to Gillian. Several unsuitable replies occurred to her, but, perhaps fortunately, she was not given the opportunity to employ any of them. Greenwood continued, 'I'm looking forward to your lecture tomorrow. Such an interesting topic. A challenging one for you, I should have thought …yes, I'm sure it will be fascinating. Now, what will you have to drink?'

Feeling distinctly ruffled, Gillian eyed the array of bottles on the table: wine in an ice bucket, gin, whisky, sherry, soda water in a siphon, tonic. 'Wine, please.' He gave her some in a lovely, thin-stemmed glass and turned to his other guests. Gillian distanced herself by a few steps; he had meant to be disconcerting. Well, well, so the game begins already, she thought; I had better sharpen my wits. She sipped her wine and contemplated Greenwood's garden.

A wide expanse of close-cropped, somewhat desiccated lawn lay between the front of the house and the long wall that protected the garden from the road. The wall was shaded by tall trees, oaks and chestnuts of enormous girth, their leaves still the dark, dust-filmed green of late summer. Behind her, the house stood in the open, its plain lines unobscured by any greenery. The rose-garden was full of blooms, wide open and blowsy in the sun, their thorny stalks rising from ancient, gnarled bases. In the centre stood a weathered sundial. An almost imperceptible wedge of shadow lay across its face.

Beyond the roses, the lawn spread out again, running away to the shaded wall which shut off the garden from its neighbours, if any—there seemed to be a wood on the other side. Two magnificent cedars of Lebanon commanded the further reaches of the lawn. Close by ran another wall, a lower one, pierced by a wrought-iron gate through which Gillian glimpsed an orderly kitchen garden. Honeysuckle and clematis hung over the wall, and flowers grew thickly in the bed at its foot, spilling over the borders and invading the grass. Thyme crept over the gravelly path, and great bushes of rosemary and lavender pressed sweetly together below towering hollyhocks. It was a beautiful English garden, eschewing rigid formality and lurid displays of colour, its faded harmonies contriving to look almost natural. This other Eden, Gillian thought, disarmed. Then Greenwood glided towards her and refilled her glass.

'Do you like gardens? Americans are never interested in flowers.'

'This garden is wonderful. You just need to tidy it up a bit and add a few straight rows of something colourful— gladioli, perhaps,' said Gillian sweetly.

'Indeed,' said Greenwood and gave her a sharp glance. He gestured towards the cedars. 'The trees are the essential element, of course. A splendid garden without trees is inconceivable. As a rule, I prefer native trees in country gardens, but one has to make an exception for cedars of Lebanon. Have you seen the magnificent specimens in the cloister at Salisbury? It was an Oxford man who was almost certainly the first to raise cedars of Lebanon in England: the Reverend Edward Pococke, a rector in Berkshire at the time. That was in the sixteen-forties. You can still see the fig tree he planted at Christ Church. Of course, the English garden really came into its own in the eighteenth century...such a dull, pathetic, feeble sort of place this garden would be without the chestnuts and oaks, don't you agree? They are older than America—if that nation sprang forth in seventeen-seventy-six, as its own citizens aver. I am particularly partial to oaks. The history of this country was hewn from the great trunks of English oaks. Now the government shrouds the land with forests of conifers in regimented rows. What sort of history can a country planted with softwoods hope for?'

It was not a question that required an answer, and Gillian made none. She was wondering whether Greenwood planted oak trees for some future man of wisdom to contemplate or whether he merely enjoyed what had been given him by someone who had lived in an age that he would have much preferred to his own.

'Softwoods,' Greenwood said scornfully. 'Houses that won't last forty years, when mean cottages have lasted four hundred. And the cities—towering monuments to the plastics industry boasting sumptuous views of other such monuments.'

Gillian made a wry face. 'I'm afraid that's a description of my office.'

'And of many others, though not here, as yet. It isn't possible to do one's best work in a building that resembles a block of council flats. So it's hardly surprising that virtually no one is *writing* history these days. I find the Americans are especially unreadable. Longwinded prose pasted together with neologisms fished out of the scrap heap of sociology. Something useful might be refined from such effluent, but history that one cannot read is not history.' Greenwood shot her a glance filled with malice and amusement.

Gillian, a prey to the particular fury that arises from having one's own views rendered thoroughly unpalatable, wanted to hit him. Then she realized with an inward laugh that this was precisely the reaction predicted by Bee. This restored her balance of temper. She replied, 'Well, I suppose I think of it as rather like medicine: the best people practise it as an art with scientific underpinnings. But plenty of sound work is done at a mundane level, and that work is necessary.'

'You are too kind. A charming fault, of course, but one that we cannot afford if history is not to be annihilated by battalions of illiterates wielding computers. The collection of data has become a substitute for thought.'

'But what about those who think clearly and well, but who haven't the gift of inspired expression?'

Greenwood smiled. 'Like the poor, they have always been with us.—Ah. I see that Victor has arrived. Forgive me.' He set down his glass and sauntered away.

Gillian buried her nose in her glass, seeking solace in the excellent hock. Don't grapple, she admonished herself, you'll never find a handhold on that surface. She drifted over to Bee and Toby. 'You were perfectly right,' she said. 'My thoughts have turned to violence already.'

CHAPTER 3

They faced about to inspect the new arrival. A battered blue
Morris 1000 had pulled in behind Bee and Toby's car, and
Greenwood was shepherding a short, dark-haired man across
the lawn. Victor Smallbone, an historian from the University
of East Anglia, a newish concrete institution outside Norwich,
was spending the weekend in Cambridge after giving lectures
at Trinity and Peterhouse. He shook Gillian's hand limply
and then ignored her, preferring to cultivate Toby. He was
smooth and plump and epicene, and he talked with animated
cleverness, waving his fat, pale fingers and tossing back a
lock of hair that strayed repeatedly into his heavy-lidded,
protuberant eyes. He had an amphibious quality, a sheen of
sweat exuding like slime over his pallid flesh, words streaming
forth like gelatinous clusters of frog spawn into the waiting,
buoyant air.

Gillian glanced across at Bee, who returned the look with
interest. In unspoken accord, they moved a little away from
the men, now joined by Greenwood, who had brought Victor
a gin and tonic. They were barely out of earshot, admiring
some enormous creamy pink roses, when Bee muttered,
'What a twit.'

'Shh. He's just displaying his wares. He wants a job.'

'He's got a job. Besides, this place doesn't need more
neutered toms. What did Greenwood say to you, by the way?'

'Nothing indictable, exactly. But why am I here? Why wasn't I merely invited to dine in college?'

'For the same reason we're all here. Professor Greenwood likes being lord of the manor. He's quite the peacock, in his way. Perhaps he wants to spread his tail feathers for you.'

'The operative word being feathers, not tail, I'm sure,' Gillian said sardonically. Bee began to laugh and then stopped suddenly as another car came up the drive. Gillian caught sight of a tan Jaguar sedan before it slid to a stop on the far side of Bee's rusty red Mini.

'Bloody hell,' said Bee under her breath.

'What's the matter?'

'Just someone I don't particularly want to run into here.'

A woman had shut the door of the sedan and was striding towards them over the grass. She was as tall as Gillian and perhaps a little younger. Her hair was cropped short, springing up from the roots in vigorous, honey-coloured curls. Her skin was honey-coloured too, tanned and opaque, and her deep-set eyes, fringed with sandy lashes, were blue-green, so that she reminded Gillian of sea and sand. At fifty yards, she might have been mistaken for a Californian, but a closer view revealed first a certain irregularity of feature and then an air of intensity overlaid with reserve that expunged any idea of the kind. She wore a crisp white cotton shirt and black linen trousers; she moved with precision and confidence over what was clearly familiar ground.

Greenwood walked a short distance to greet her. 'Pamela, my dear.' He brought her to Gillian and Bee. 'This is Pamela Ditton, a zoologist at King's, and my cousin. Gillian Adams, an historian who is on sabbatical leave in London this year. And Bee—Toby Fox's wife—you know, of course.'

'How do you do?' Pamela said to Gillian. Then, 'Hullo, Bee.'

'Hullo, Pamela,' Bee said gruffly. Gillian was asking herself whether Greenwood had intended to annoy Bee or whether that was how he thought of her. Toby and Victor ambled towards them, and Greenwood finished the introductions and went to fetch Pamela a glass of wine. Victor was still talking fluently, Toby seemed restive, and Bee was fidgety. Pamela looked attentively at Gillian, as if shutting the others out, and asked whether she had been in Cambridge before.

'Yes. I was a research student at Newnham in the Sixties,' Gillian said.

'Were you? I was here then too—at Girton. Such a nuisance it was, being so far from the centre of Cambridge. Actually, I wanted to do my research in Oxford, if only to annoy Alistair, but the best man in my field happened to be here.'

'What's your particular interest?' Gillian inquired, wishing to know why Greenwood would have been annoyed, but not liking to ask just at that moment.

'Animal behaviour. Elephants, to be precise. I'm interested in whether they can survive in the wild, given the increasing pressure of Africa's human population.'

'It must look pretty grim, with high prices for ivory on the one hand, and a baby boom on the other.'

'Yes. And the desert is creeping south each year. Lots of factors come into it, but if elephants survive, it will be because man permits it. And so we must know what they need.'

'Do you spend a lot of time in Africa?' Gillian asked. It was easy to imagine this lean, brown woman tramping through the bush.

'Yes. I spend about three months a year in Kenya. An uncle of mine—not on Alistair's side, the other one—has a farm in the highlands, which helps. I can leave all my gear there, for one thing. I've done a lot of work in Tsavo. That's difficult country for man and beast: hot, waterless, thorny scrub. Hardly anyone goes into parts of it—except poachers.'

'Don't you worry about them? They're dangerous people.'

'Yes, they are. But most of them know me by now, and know where I am. They don't bother me.'

'What about the animals? Mightn't you be eaten by a lion sometime?' Victor asked, sounding faintly hopeful.

'I'm not alone there; I always have a couple of Africans with me.' Pamela smiled. 'Besides, I'm a passable shot.'

'She wasted her youth potting pheasants,' Greenwood said, coming up and handing her a glass. 'I shouldn't worry about her, Victor, she'd probably eat the lion.' He turned to Gillian. 'Don't encourage her. Once she starts talking about Africa, there's no stopping her. Pamela has certain enthusiasms which require pruning.'

He said it lightly, but there was a cutting edge to the remark. Pamela gave him a venomous look. 'Anyhow, my dear,' he went on blandly, 'Gillian is an historian of the British Empire, so she already knows whatever is worth knowing about Africa.' Having thus neatly blown up two targets with one projectile, he briefly held his fire.

Bee finished off her gin with reckless speed and observed that it was a hot day for October.

'Frightfully hot,' agreed Victor. 'The steamy tropics of Cambridgeshire—one expects to see bougainvillea festooning the Elizabethan walls. And here we stand in the midday sun, dressed as if we were setting an example to the natives.'

Hardly, thought Gillian. Victor was looking rather damp about the hairline, and from the armpits of his blazer there rose, like invisible steam, the acrid stench of aged sweat.

'October would be my favourite month if it weren't for the influx of undergraduates,' said Toby. 'All those fresh young faces depress me.'

'There's May—all those soft, lush, delicate shades of green. Even the drive to London is pretty then,' Bee offered.

'Too fecund,' replied Toby, curling his lip. Greenwood's penetrating but uninterested gaze swept over them impartially, then he set about replenishing the drinks.

'Alistair still thinks of Africa as the Dark Continent,' said Pamela, glaring after him.

'And what's he got against Oxford?' Gillian asked. 'I should have thought he'd be perfectly matched to its opulence.'

'That's just it,' Pamela said with an engaging grin. 'Everyone always said so, and Alistair hates to be predictable.'

'So he came here instead.'

'Where else?'

Where else indeed, Gillian thought. In her mind, he was inextricably linked with Cambridge.

'You're American, aren't you.' It was a statement.

'Partly. I'm an American-Canadian hybrid, both by birth and education. I grew up in New England.'

'Where do you teach?'

'In Vancouver. The University of the Pacific Northwest.'

'Vancouver? That's a beautiful place, I've been told.'

'I'm sure you have.' Gillian sighed. 'The mountains and the sea,' she intoned. 'That's the native litany. Oh, the ineluctable grandeur. I'd trade all the mountains and every last evergreen on them for a little, rounded New England hill, a bit of stone wall and a few bare branches of an oak tree.' She smiled. 'Or for almost any piece of countryside in England—except the fens and the dreary broads.'

'I'm always torn. I've never seen a landscape as magnificent as East Africa's, but I can't leave England for long without yearning for little domesticated fields and broach spires and the Fellows' Garden.'

There came a sound of wheels on gravel, and everyone looked up to see a fiery red Lagonda shoot out from beneath the trees and halt, panting, in the drive.

'Oh. It's Denham,' said Pamela. 'Quite a little family gathering.'

'Denham?'

'Alistair's brother. His older brother, though no one ever believes it. He lives in London.'

'Is he an academic too?' asked Gillian.

'Heavens, no. He's not the type—not at all. Not like Alistair a bit. Denham's a capitalist. He shuffles money around and it multiplies. You'll—' She broke off. 'My God. Who is that?' An apparition had emerged from the Lagonda and was approaching them in Denham's wake. It was a tall girl, dressed all in black. Her hair stood out from her head as if caught in a fierce wind, and it was dyed dead black, except for a wide magenta strip down one side. Her dress floated around her body in random gypsy layers of dusky chiffon trimmed with something that glittered dully, like steel. 'Jesus,' muttered Bee. 'She looks like the wicked fairy.'

The dress left a lot of her bare: arms, shoulders, and a considerable expanse of breast, but she wore sheer black stockings, stiletto-heeled shoes decorated with silver spurs, and black lace gloves. Above her fierce hair bobbed two shining silver balls atop slender springs, like Venusian antennae. In the distance her face was a pale oval with two dark hollows for eyes, but as she drew closer Gillian took in more details: enormous violet eyes decorated with elaborate black stripes, and two tiny circles of black lace pasted to her cheekbone. Her dress was trimmed with grommets; they glinted and clattered as she walked. Over her shoulder hung a small, black leather bag, swinging as if heavily weighted. She had the marvellous, lit-up skin of a twenty-year-old; against the deep black of her dress and hair it was pure cream, as if she had been dipped in it. They all stared in rude wonder as she sauntered towards them, insolent, expensive, and so overtly sexual that Gillian sensed, nearby, male flesh contracting. In the pastel tranquillity of Greenwood's garden, the girl looked as incongruous as a bizarre, incandescent fish from the depths of the sea, one of those that occasionally appear in the daily catch and startle fishermen with visions of another, stranger world. 'Wow!' thought Gillian inelegantly. It occurred to her that Denham Greenwood, if unlike his brother, must at least share with him a propensity for disconcerting his fellow man. She tore her eyes from his dark lady and looked at him. Alistair Greenwood had gone to meet him, and the two of them were walking side by side across the sunlit lawn. They were much of a height, and Denham's pale hair and beaky nose repeated his brother's.

But Denham's hair had thinned over the high pink dome of his forehead, and living well had left more of a mark. His excellent clothes did not entirely conceal a somewhat fleshy middle, and the angular bone structure that in Alistair was all but skeletal, was in Denham softened and padded. It was the eyes that were most unlike, however. Denham's were not grey but blue, a pale receding blue like an uncertain spring sky. They were shrewd enough, but he did not possess his brother's unnerving gaze. And he did look younger, Gillian saw; it was doubtless the effect of more flesh on the bones.

As the trio approached the rest of the guests, the little group around Gillian was bereft of conversation. Greenwood's face was inscrutable as he performed the introductions. It entered her mind that the luncheon was developing an unexpected potential for high comedy.

'My brother Denham,' said Greenwood to the assembly, 'who has brought—er—Fiona Clay.' Denham shook hands and smiled affably; Fiona gave them a single distant nod, as though she had already written them off as a collective bore. She accepted a gin and tonic and lit a cigarette. Apparently feeling no need to lubricate the frozen social gears, she stared at nothing in particular and did not speak.

At a larger gathering, a low buzzing, as of ill-natured bees, would have been discernible, but among only eight people, nothing could be said. A barbed silence quivered momentarily among them. Gillian stole a quick look at Greenwood. He was scrutinizing Fiona, and, for a brief moment, his habitually sardonic and detached expression gave way to one of outrage. Gillian thought she understood: the rude world had breached his walls. As Fiona stood there, indifferent, the surroundings seemed to shrink around her; she occupied the garden like an army of the future.

Then the logjam of unvoiced reactions broke; conversation began again. Denham, whom Gillian suspected of enjoying the sensation his companion had caused, made short work of a large drink. He told his brother that he had brought a case of wine. 'Quite remarkable, actually; I picked up several cases at an auction last week; some poor bastard had a dozen bottles of Château d'Yquem nineteen-forty-seven sitting in his cellar and died before he drank them.'

'You may be sure I won't,' Alistair Greenwood replied. 'Do stow them in the cellar, will you, I must see to my guests.' Denham nodded and walked back to his car. A minute later, Gillian saw him disappear around the far side of the house carrying a carton with extreme care.

Meanwhile, Toby and Victor began to talk about the government's education cuts, and Bee asked Gillian about a London friend, leaving Pamela a choice of Fiona or her cousin. She chose her cousin, or rather he chose her, refilling her glass and remarking quite audibly, 'You're a little morose, my dear. Pining for your wilderness again? I cannot imagine why.'

'I know you can't. But as it happens I wasn't. I was merely wishing I hadn't come to lunch.'

'How discourteous of you to say so. Farouche.' Greenwood smiled a charming smile. 'But then, why not? You have already—so to speak—stubbed your toe, haven't you?'

Gillian wondered what he could possibly mean. Pamela seemed to know.

'Damn you, Alistair.'

'My dear, Cambridge, unlike Africa, is small. Also, unlike Africa, it is civilized. You must try to remember that.'

'Perhaps I should stay in Africa,' Pamela said coldly.

'Oh, I shouldn't do that. The insects will devour your heirlooms.'

Pamela turned and strode away through the roses and became temporarily absorbed in the beauties of the herbaceous border. Bee's eyes followed her. Then Denham emerged from a door on the near side of the house, and Fiona, black chiffon swaying about her thighs, stalked across the lawn to meet him.

'What is she doing here?' Bee marvelled. Toby joined them. 'Waste of a beautiful girl, if you ask me,' he said disparagingly. 'Still, I suppose it's an interesting cultural phenomenon.'

'A phenomenon, certainly,' said Greenwood, 'but hardly interesting. The worst aspect of modern barbarism is that it is so dull.'

'Apparently your brother doesn't agree with you,' Toby replied, smirking a little.

'Our views seldom coincide,' Greenwood said coldly. It was a snub. 'Still, she's English—one must be grateful for small mercies. These days, London is so overrun with the ragtag and bobtail of the world's distant and unruly parts, that I should be quite prepared for a Hottentot. You need not look outraged, I was not referring to you,' he said parenthetically to Gillian. 'You're more English than she is, in the sense I mean.'

'Thanks a lot.'

'And it is not, need I say, a vulgar matter of colour. It is simply that England will be destroyed if it is allowed to become a melting pot for other countries. Consider the fate of your continent. Its crudity derives not just from its youth, but from the indigestible hodge-podge of migratory elements.' He turned to Toby. 'I'm sure you would hold the view that although England no longer rules an empire, nor claims to be a great power, there remains something worth defending. And Cambridge, if I may put it so, is a place to stand.'

'Quite. I was saying to Gillian only this morning that our standards must be maintained—'

'Precisely. And standards of admission are critical. I do not conceive it to be a part of our duty to educate inadequate students, whatever their claims upon our interest or sympathy. In particular, foreign and Commonwealth students—those from such places as Hong Kong—must be carefully screened. Don't you think so?'

Toby stared at him. 'I—I—yes, of course.'

'Excellent. I was certain you would understand my point.' His glance fell upon Bee. 'You, I suppose, think differently.'

Next victim, thought Gillian. But why was Toby looking so shaken?

'I'm not in favour of lowering academic standards, if that's what you mean,' said Bee shortly.

'Naturally not. No one is. But the pursuit of other goals may have precisely that effect.'

'Such as the admission of women? You're opposed to women in men's colleges.'

'Nonsense.'

'Would you object to the admission of women to Peterhouse?'

'I would accept it. But the issue has taken an unfortunate direction, and as a result the women's colleges are suffering. They were established only a century ago and have struggled against terrible disadvantages. And now they are being undermined because the best women students will often choose the men's colleges—for good financial or geographical or aesthetic reasons. Moreover, the women's colleges are now hiring men, and as a consequence there are fewer places for women.'

'I find it so instructive that the same sort of person who used to oppose the existence of women's colleges now becomes their most vigorous defender. They were once seen as invaders of the male preserve; now that your backs are to the wall, they have become your last hope.'

'Rubbish. The presence of qualified women cannot but be advantageous. It is merely that change for the sake of change must be avoided, as must political expediency. We in Cambridge have the luxury of being able to rise above expediency. We should use it well. Toby, another drink?'

As Greenwood left the little knot of guests, Pamela rejoined it. Gillian, waiting warily for Greenwood's enfilade to resume, drank more wine and commented on it to Pamela.

'Oh, Denham gives it to Alistair,' was the indifferent reply.

'Really? I thought it was probably from the college cellar.'

'Denham is a connoisseur. Wine, cigars, women, cars. He goes to auctions and is a frightful show-off at dinner parties. He always brings Alistair some of his spectacular bottles.'

'That's generous of him.'

'I wouldn't call it generosity.'

'Does he always bring his spectacular women, too?' inquired Bee. 'What about Fiona? What auction did he find her at?'

'Oh, Denham's been slumming again.' Pamela sounded amused. 'He's a vulgar little man, really, in spite of his upbringing.'

'She looks more like a circus performer than someone at Sunday lunch in the country,' said Toby. 'I hope I shan't have to sit next to her. What on earth would we talk about?'

'Try films,' said Bee. 'She's probably a nice little thing from Hammersmith who wants to be an actress.'

'Perhaps you needn't talk at all. She hasn't said a word yet,' Victor observed. 'Possibly deaf-mutes are the *dernier cri* in some London circles.'

'Oh, she undoubtedly has an appalling accent,' replied Toby.

Here they go, thought Gillian. In a minute they'll be pulling apart her accent and her vocabulary—if she has any—and trying to figure out whether her parents are grocers. They were quite unblushing about it, and Gillian knew that to comment would be to invite a lecture on the class system in America. And who was she to comment? Denham made her recoil, too. Starting with the Guccis and working upwards to the aftershave, he had the international, impersonal quality of certain hotel chains. He was 'continental'—as the word was applied to certain restaurants in middle America. She was repelled by him, and—there was no getting around it— she was a snob.

As for Fiona, Gillian had begun to feel sorry for her, wishing that the girl were as invulnerable as she had appeared at the outset. At another sort of gathering, larger and more formal (or less) her silence might have sustained an element of fascination, inaccessible and cool, but in the small, conversational compass of this group, it was unnatural and a signal of suffering. Denham shouldn't have brought her.

Fiona stayed close to him, walking a little unsteadily as her sharp heels sank into the turf. He made her another drink, and they approached the gossiping cluster of guests, necessitating a sudden shift of topic. Pamela turned to Gillian and asked, 'When and where are you lecturing tomorrow? I'd like to come if I can.'

'In the Chetwynd Room at King's; I don't know exactly what time I'm supposed to speak, but tea is served first, at about four o'clock.'

'Can you find your way there?' inquired Greenwood, who had returned with another bottle of wine.

'Oh yes. It's just off King's Lane, isn't it?'

'That's right. May I meet you there at four, then?'

'That would be fine.'

'Four o'clock,' said Pamela. 'I don't think I'm free then, unfortunately. Tell me what you're working on.'

As Gillian talked, she saw Fiona take out a cigarette and fumble for a light. Toby found a match and lit it, and she leaned towards him, an edge of pink nipple showing at the loose neckline of her dress. The match quivered a little; Toby's temples were beaded with sweat.

Then Greenwood announced lunch.

CHAPTER 4

It was an incompatible little group that sat down together. Greenwood was at the head of the table with Gillian on his right; he had put Denham at the foot, flanked by Fiona and Pamela. Gillian had Toby on her other side, which was far from satisfactory, but then she didn't want to sit next to any of the other men either. Bee, across from her, was sandwiched between Greenwood and the neutered tom, which presumably afforded her pleasure equal to Gillian's own. Gillian glanced down the table to see how Pamela liked sitting across from Fiona, but Pamela's attention was elsewhere, directed past Greenwood, whose back was to the door through which they had come. Gillian turned her head and saw, hanging to the left of the door, a truly splendid picture. A tame green landscape receded into a summery distance, clouds drifted over meadow and copse, and in the sunlit foreground a spirited grey horse was poised, caught in mid-stride and placed like an idol in a green shrine. The anatomical perfection and the Englishness were unmistakable.

'That's a magnificent Stubbs,' she said to Greenwood.

'I agree. It's a late one, painted in the seventeen-nineties when he was enjoying the patronage of the Prince Regent. Stubbs has never been sufficiently appreciated—he has been relegated to the ranks of the sporting painters when what he has given us is a superb record of country life. There's nothing sentimental about his work, and no ephemeral drama. There is, instead, *douceur de vivre.*'

'And a passionate accuracy,' said Gillian, thinking of the gruelling labour of dissection to which Stubbs had devoted himself. The grisly details were unimaginable in the presence of the distilled vision which they had in part formed, as the grubby tedium of research was invisible beneath Greenwood's Augustan prose. 'Did you ever consider being an art historian?'

'Not seriously. It's too technical a field. I prefer that my knowledge of history inform my appreciation of the arts.' A small, mischievous smile came and went. 'Anthony Blunt is unsurpassed in that subject.' He sipped his wine and waited.

'Are you expecting a moral outburst? How can a man like that be explained? A scholar of immaculate integrity who engages in the sordid trickery of spying? An extraordinary Janus. What do you think?'

'What is integrity in the political arena? And the evidence is tainted. If one is to use the word sordid, it may as well be applied to the process of exposure and concealment that has enveloped the affair since the first suspicion fell on him. To believe in the Soviet Union during the Stalinist era amounts to wilful political naïveté, but at what exact point that becomes a form of corruption I shouldn't care to say without weighing the evidence. What is certain is that his scholarship stands untouched. That is what will endure.'

But what does it mean, Gillian wanted to ask, what does it mean to be a superb scholar and a shrivelled human being? Why does it happen? She struggled to formulate the question, to find an acceptable terminology, but she could not, and the moment passed swiftly by, washed away by succeeding wavelets of conversation.

The housekeeper brought in the first course, leek soup in a silver tureen, and Greenwood turned his attention to Victor Smallbone, who had asked him about a collection of rare books owned by a fellow of Corpus Christi.

A sense of peace and well-being seeped into Gillian. The room, brought to life by human voices and the gentle clinking of silver on china, was serenely beautiful. They sat at a long table covered with a white cloth, in the centre of which stood a great crystal bowl of enormous pale yellow roses, their *fin de siècle* petals heavy with tomorrow's decay. Amber sconces cast a faint radiance on the dark oak wainscoting, and in the afternoon light from the tall windows the meadow Stubbs had painted nearly two centuries earlier took on the fleeting, luminous green of the first days of full summer.

The others seemed to feel the spell too, chatting gently and pleasantly enough, all, that is, with the exception of Fiona, who finished off her gin and then drank her wine, hardly touching the soup. She spoke to Denham once or twice, but receiving only a perfunctory response gave up and sat in ungracious silence. She must be getting rather drunk, thought Gillian, and Denham, having made his point by bringing her, has abandoned her. She could hear snatches of Denham's talk; he was telling Pamela and Toby about the intricacies of the London property market.

Now and then the various conversations at the table meshed, then they flowed separately again. The talk fluttered from one thing to another: British Rail, the economy, the Common Market and those nasty French apples, the Booker Prize, the fate of *The Times*, the fate of Poland. Once, in response to a cynical aside of Greenwood's, Gillian said, 'But don't you then feel a stifled passion to act—to redirect the course of events?'

'Only limited forms of action are possible, otherwise one compromises one's position. One cannot be both participant and incorruptible observer. I would remind you that all governments are incipient tyrannies.'

After the soup, there was cold poached salmon, glazed and prettily re-armoured in scales of paper-thin cucumber, and then roast duckling, accompanied by a Chambolle-Musigny and a discussion of the Pope's possible visit to

Britain. Gillian enjoyed this part of the lunch particularly. The duck and the wine were wonderful, and Greenwood, in top form, treated his assembled guests to an elegant, malicious and authoritative discourse on the Church of Rome, not omitting one or two caustic excursions into Anglican orthodoxies. He was pungently anticlerical, but his merciless wit made no allowance for ignorance, and of all his listeners only Victor, who as it turned out was in church history and was writing a book on the recurrent theme of the Popish Plot in English history, was able to follow every reference. The rest of the academics galloped along behind, missing the odd hurdle, but enjoying themselves. Denham, however, looked stonily at his plate, and Fiona, apparently deciding that the only thing to do when faced with such an intimidating flow of eloquence was to drink, finished her wine and when her glass was not refilled helped herself to Denham's. He made an embarrassed, furtive attempt to retrieve it but failed. Greenwood, observing this, said, 'I'm sure she would prefer gin. Why don't you make her another?'

The flicker of contempt could not be missed; Denham turned a dull crimson, and Fiona clumsily set down the glass. Wine sloshed over the brim, and a shocking red flood spread across the white damask. There was a frozen little pause while Denham righted the glass and dabbed ineffectively with his napkin. Gillian picked up the heavy silver salt cellar and passed it to Toby, who looked at her uncertainly. 'Pour it on the stain,' she muttered. Obediently, he emptied it, and for a few seconds everyone watched the red liquid seeping noiselessly through the crystals.

In the silence, Fiona made her first audible remark. She was concise.

'Fucking bastard.'

Her elbows were braced on the table, and in her right hand was a small but real pistol, the business end pointing straight at Greenwood's chest.

Paralysis struck. No one could move or speak, and Fiona held the stage with unsmiling, feline poise. So it remained for a moment; then, her eyes glittering, she swept the empty glass from the table with a violent, contemptuous movement of her arm, and they heard the fragile stem snap. Her gaze stayed fixed upon Greenwood, but it became an unfocused glare, as if she had begun to forget what she was looking at. Then her lips moved in an effort to speak that loosened her concentration on the gun. It drooped momentarily, and Pamela's arm shot out. She grasped Fiona's wrist with swift brutality, slamming it on the table. The gun went off, deafeningly.

In the centre of the table, the large crystal bowl of roses broke, flooding the cloth with water and petals. An instantaneous splintering thud came from behind Gillian, who yelped involuntarily and ducked. Greenwood didn't move. Fiona tore her wrist free from Pamela's grip, dropping the gun, which clattered across the table and dropped over the side, landing with a muffled thump on the dense carpet. Gillian saw a scorched hole in the tablecloth. She looked at Greenwood, whose face, drained of blood, was a pasty grey like recycled paper.

'Are you all right?' she whispered.

He turned his head towards her, and, as though the movement had released a tourniquet, the colour began to come back to his face. 'Perfectly intact, thank you.' For a moment, he said nothing more, gathering his forces. Then the onslaught came. He looked straight down the table at Denham, who was staring glassily back at him, and said, 'This has been a disgraceful piece of vulgar exhibitionism from beginning to end. You have contrived to stain this occasion with the cheap and violent character of an episode on the television. Remove this Hun and return her to whatever unspeakable world she customarily inhabits.' The words fell like separate chips of ice through the still air.

Then he turned to Pamela, who had picked up the gun and was examining it with professional interest. 'Give me

that contemptible object. I will see that it is disposed of.'
She handed it to him without a word. The danger had passed,
but shock held the rest of them in their places, rendering the
disparate stiffness of their natures pliable and uniform,
slowing speech and thought. They watched Greenwood,
mesmerized, as he carried the gun, holding it like something
not only deadly but infectious—a vial of plague bacilli,
perhaps—to the massive mahogany sideboard. This was an
elaborate piece of furniture, with many doors and drawers,
and gilded handles. Opening one of the lower doors, he
exposed three more small drawers, each ornamented by a tiny
lock. He took a key from the middle lock, placed the gun in
the drawer, locked it, pulled a key-ring from his pocket and
attached the little golden key. Then he straightened and stood
in a deliberate attitude, waiting for Denham and Fiona to depart.

Denham got heavily to his feet. Fiona, still sitting, gave a
little moan. Then she fell forward, and her head hit the table.

'Oh Christ, she's passed out,' said Pamela. She picked up
a goblet of water and dashed it in Fiona's half-turned face.
Fiona blinked. 'Bastard,' she muttered groggily as Denham
hauled her to her feet.

'What an appalling spectacle,' said Greenwood, not
moving 'Mrs. Hill will be prostrate when she sees this room.
I suppose I shall have to drive her home.'

'Do you want some help?' Gillian asked Denham.

'No. No, thank you,' he grunted, beginning to make a
graceless and unassisted exit.

'Goodbye,' said Pamela. And then the others echoed her,
ritual coming rather comically to the rescue, covering the
tracks of chaos. Denham, half-carrying Fiona out of the room,
muttered something inaudible.

'I hope she's sick all over the Lagonda,' Toby remarked
when they had gone.

Gillian twisted in her chair and looked at the wall behind
her. The bullet had embedded itself, splintering the
wainscoting a little below and well to the left of the Stubbs.

She surveyed the mess on the table. Water and flowers were everywhere, the water mingling with the wine and salt, spreading a pink tinge through the cloth. It wasn't much, she reflected, considering what might have happened. But in this harmonious, stately room, the shards of crystal winking among the smashed roses were sufficient emblems of savagery.

Greenwood was still standing by the sideboard. He glanced at Pamela. 'I believe I've forgotten to say thank you.' She shook her head. 'And now,' he went on, 'I think we should retire to the garden. It will be more pleasant to take coffee there.' He shepherded them out of the room and back the way they had come to the bright openness of the rose-garden, where the westering sun was nearing the tops of the oak trees.

'Aren't you going to call the police?' Gillian asked.

'Certainly not,' he replied, so forbiddingly that she said nothing more. 'I must go and inquire about the coffee. Mrs. Hill may be cowering in the scullery.' He went back into the house.

His departure released a nervous spate of conversation. 'You certainly kept your head,' Gillian said to Pamela.

'I had to—couldn't have her waving that pistol about. She might have missed Alistair and put a hole in the Stubbs.'

'She almost did.'

'Yes. My timing was imperfect.'

'Why doesn't he call the police?'

'Because he'd prefer not.'

'But—'

'Don't meddle,' Pamela said succinctly.

A faint clanking was heard, and Greenwood emerged from the house, bearing a heavy silver tray. 'The coffee, fortunately, was just ready.' He set it down. 'Mrs. Hill was three rooms away in the scullery with the tap full on; she thought she'd heard a car backfiring in the lane. I'm afraid the havoc inside has indeed upset her; I'll take her home in a few minutes.'

'What did you tell her?' inquired Victor, a little nervously.

'That there had been an accident. And that one of the guests had become ill and had to be taken home.'

'Did she believe you?' inquired Pamela.

Greenwood smiled. 'Probably not. But she has been in my employment for more than fifteen years. She does not gossip about my affairs.'

The implication hung in the air as he poured coffee from a silver pot into tiny, gold-rimmed cups. They were not to gossip either. 'Do stay,' he urged pleasantly. 'I shan't be long, and we mustn't allow this preposterous incident to destroy the afternoon.' They accepted the little cups uncomfortably. 'Perhaps you'd care to explore the garden,' he added. Taking this as a polite dismissal, or possibly as a release from surveillance, the guests began to drift away, carrying their cups. 'Have you had your fill of Cambridge libraries?' he asked Gillian. 'Or would you like to see mine?'

'Please.'

'I shall have to go, Alistair,' said Pamela. 'I have to give a lecture tomorrow morning, and I'll be out all evening, so I must finish it now.' The three of them walked towards the house. 'Well,' she continued when they were out of earshot of the others, 'that was a singular guest list even for you, Alistair. Fiona wasn't your doing, but why on earth was that horrid little man Smallbone invited?'

'He's an old student of mine, and he's applying for a job here. He shan't get it, however. I'll see to that.'

'I'm sure you will. Goodbye, Gillian,' she said as they neared the door. 'Don't bother, Alistair, I'll let myself out. Thank you for lunch. It was gratifying to see that Cambridge and Africa aren't as dissimilar as you thought.' She marched down the hall as Greenwood led Gillian into the library, a spacious room with windows facing south and west towards the garden.

'You will have a macabre impression of Cambridge life, I fear. But perhaps, being American, you take these events in your stride. An acquaintance of mine who has been at Berkeley for some years tells me that at the sound of gunfire he merely goes on opening his letters. Here, we haven't the need to become accustomed to such things. And we strive against the odds to preserve the remnants of a civilized life.'

Indeed, thought Gillian, looking around the room with a sharp pang of envy. The library was tall and cool, lapped in shadow, its faded, ice-blue silk curtains half drawn across the windows. It contained a large writing-table, several deep armchairs, a fireplace over which hung a portrait of a Victorian gentleman—undoubtedly a progenitor of Greenwood's, as the nose and ears were clearly recognizable— a set of oak library steps, and the books. Oak shelves lined three of the walls. Leather and gilt gleamed, row upon row, from polished floor to coffered ceiling.

Greenwood waved a hand casually at his treasury. 'Take down anything you like. My collection does not include books that cannot be read.'

As they walked further into the room, Gillian saw a delicate Queen Anne table at the far end, laden with several massive volumes. Greenwood picked one up and handed it to her. It was a volume of *The Decline and Fall of the Roman Empire*, superbly bound in quarto. 'These belonged to Gibbon himself. I leave you with a beguiling companion.' Then he went out, closing the door behind him.

For a moment, Gillian hardly dared to breathe near the book. She opened it with caution, the paper rich and heavy under her fingers as she turned the pages. Her eye fell upon a random line: '…the most splendid appellations have been frequently lavished on the most inconsiderable objects.' She smiled. The Regius Professor would be entirely at home in these pages.

She wandered along the shelves, curious and admiring. There were books in Latin, Greek, German, French and Italian, but evidently her host did not read Russian or Mandarin; the books on the Soviet Union and China, like those on India, were English. Drifting happily on this literary sea, Gillian had a Toynbee-ish vision of empires rising and crumbling again into nothing. A hundred glittering dynasties were chronicled here, their sages remembered, their policies assessed, their wealth and wit and decline recalled, dissected, explained. Philosophers, essayists, novelists and poets crowded the shelves in a dignified throng. Erasmus and Montaigne were probable favourites, she thought, and, among the novelists, Trollope. What was not there was the twentieth century, except its history. The two world wars, America, communism, they were present, but thought and literature and art disappeared, as if the lamps that had gone out all over Europe had never been relit.

She twitched back a curtain and looked out at the garden, where the trees now cast long shadows over the lawn. The roses swayed in a breath of wind, and a few petals fluttered to the ground. On the table, the coffee-pot stood in lonely splendour amid the abandoned cups. The guests were nowhere to be seen.

She left the library and, succumbing to curiosity, peeped into the dining-room, where the table had been cleared and all the debris swept away. The scene at lunch had been utterly effaced, but for a small hole in the wall. The hole struck her as looking slightly different. She walked over and peered at it more closely. The bullet had been removed.

Just then she heard, faintly, the scrunch of wheels on gravel. Greenwood was returning, no doubt. She went into the hall and through the sitting-room which gave on to the garden. There she found Bee, reclining on a sofa and apparently rather the worse for wear. She was quite pale.

'I've been sick,' she said in a low voice. 'Don't tell anyone. Too much booze in the hot sun, I guess.'

'Your secret is safe with me. But you'd better come out now, if you can. I heard a car in the drive.'

They went out and joined Toby, who was standing disconsolately among the roses. 'It's time we went home,' he said. Gillian, too, longed to go.

'Seen enough of the garden, have you?' Bee asked.

Toby shrugged. 'There's a charming little tennis court tucked away among the trees. I wonder if he uses it.'

Then Victor came round the corner of the house. 'Professor Greenwood is back. I've been contemplating the winsome eccentricities of the English country house. You should have come round past the old stables; the Elizabethan structure is seen to best advantage from that direction. I say, what do you suppose he intends to do?'

'I don't know,' replied Bee, who was still looking quite wan, 'but I should like to go home now.'

As she finished speaking, Greenwood came briskly across the lawn. Though all four guests were eager to leave, he brought the afternoon to an unhurried close, and another half hour had passed before they found themselves driving sedately down the lane. It was only 4:30, but Gillian felt as though she had been at Camford House for days.

CHAPTER 5

When Gillian awoke the next morning, her first thought was: do I have a hangover? After leaving Greenwood's house late on Sunday afternoon, she had spent the tailend of the day in Bee's dreary sitting-room drinking whisky and talking over the bizarre adventure they had shared. Fascinating as the matter was, Gillian had found herself seeking to divert the conversation to other channels. Something in Toby's tense, irritable excitement and Bee's glib maledictions had repelled her, and, understandably, they had been unable to leave the subject. They talk too much, she had thought wearily. Toby had gone on and on, until Bee, too sodden with drink to stay awake, had crawled upstairs. Gillian had wanted to go to bed too, but Toby had begged her to stay a little longer. He had talked compulsively, and, as if his self-containment had sprung a series of leaks, little gouts of anger and misery and fear began to appear and run together and deepen, until it seemed to Gillian that he was sitting in a pool of despair. She was unwillingly stirred by pity, mixed with a wish that he would stop, if only because she knew that the next day he would loathe himself for speaking and her for listening.

'Bee—Christ—all she thinks about is that Cambridge has done her an injustice. What about me? I *have* a job here, and what has it done? Given me every conceivable opportunity to recognize that I fall short. It hands me the yardstick, and

I measure and measure and know that I won't grow any more. King's wouldn't have me, you know. I wanted more than anything to be a fellow of King's. But they turned me down, and for so many years I thought—bloody bastards. You didn't want me because I'm not some trendy leftist. I'll show you. But I haven't showed them a damned thing. My college has been good to me, and all I can say for myself is that I've been a good boy: I've given it all I can. And people like bloody Alistair Greenwood don't make life any easier—treating everyone else like mere mortals who have gate-crashed Mount Olympus. How do you cope, Gillian? Or aren't there any gods at your university?'

'Where they are doesn't matter. I know I'll never be an Alistair Greenwood. I guess I just do the best I can.' This had sounded so lame in her own ears that she added, 'and I try to invest some of myself elsewhere as well.'

'Where?'

She shifted uncomfortably. 'Oh, you know—in lovers and friends.'

Toby had swallowed the last of his drink and moved towards the stairs. 'I suppose I'll have a chance to try that now. What a delightful prospect.'

Gillian had gone up to her room then, her brain clouded by the whisky on top of all the good wine she had drunk that afternoon.

Once in bed, she had been seized by a fractious sleeplessness, so she had sat up late re-reading *Lucia*, which she had brought upstairs from the sitting-room in case of need. She hadn't found Bee's selection of bedside literature particularly soothing; it consisted of Simone de Beauvoir's book on Sartre's final decline, a volume of Anaïs Nin's diaries, *Flying*, and the latest Doris Lessing—*Shikasta Revisited*, or something, Gillian remembered crossly. She was more in the mood for *Brideshead Revisited*, and she knew it was bound to be somewhere on Bee's shelves, but her eye had lit upon E. F. Benson, whose witty microscope might furnish some distraction.

Eventually, she had fallen into a heavy sleep, only to have awakened again at 3:00 in the morning, the body's revenge for excessive consumption of alcohol. Her thoughts swam in the darkness, enlarged and distorted as if she were thinking under water. The lunch—everything about it—seemed monstrous, utterly disconnected from both romantic Cambridge and the workaday Cambridge that carried on under, around and despite the gilded encrustations of myth.

Now, in the penumbra of early morning, protected by heavy curtains and the silence of the little street below, she tested her senses one by one, waiting for the sluggish, painful responses that would inform her that she had been idiotic enough to drink too much on the day preceding her lecture. She turned her head gently from side to side, that was all right, so she blinked and then cautiously opened her eyes. That was all right too, and she began to realize that she had miraculously escaped any undesirable consequences of Sunday's indulgence. After about five minutes during which no horrid sensations attacked her, she bravely sat upright and drew the curtains.

Light flooded the room, but it didn't hurt. She was fine, and the monsters of the night had shrunk. She still had no perspective on the events of the previous day, but that could wait. She looked out at the blank, blue sky and decided to walk about Cambridge that morning. She hadn't yet returned in any real sense; the Cambridge of her memories, the piece interlocking with the other pieces and places that made up her past, was a specific inhabited architecture, and as yet she had barely set eyes upon a stone of it. She had seen familiar faces, forms in a grotesque dance, but alone they told her little. Cambridge was, if anything, a landscape with figures.

She put on light woollen trousers, a silk shirt, a suede jacket and walking shoes. In a corner of the guest room stood a cheval glass which Bee, while still a student at Newnham, had acquired in the Portobello Road in a mad moment and then dragged back to Cambridge on the train. She had staggered triumphantly into her room, Gillian remembered, gaily scornful of her companions, who had been sure she would be forced to abandon the cumbersome object. In fact, she had told Gillian with glee, they had collectively bet £4— the price of the glass—against her successful return, so in the end she had got it for nothing.

Gillian smiled at the memory and at the streak of sentiment that must have induced Bee to cherish this relic; it blurred her harsh outline a little. She touched the smooth mahogany frame, thinking that apart from Bee's books, which she had begun collecting when she was a student, the glass was the only object Gillian had seen that belonged to their shared past, to the Cambridge she was setting out to find that morning.

She looked at herself before going downstairs. At forty, she had an air of battered elegance, a lean, efficient grace, like a seasoned clipper ship. She was tall and slight, the flesh economical and smooth over long bones, and she saw herself in black and white: features finely cut, as in an engraving, grey eyes, dark hair. She hadn't altered much in the last five years, she thought; she looked tired more often—the lines at the corners of her eyes had deepened a little—and there were some silvery threads in the soft, charcoal mass of hair.

Sometime after they had met two years earlier, Edward had told her that she reminded him of a picture of Athene in a book of myths he had read in his childhood. This had pleased her immensely, and, remembering it, she had later bought a white *crêpe-de-chine* gown in a vaguely Grecian style which suited her admirably. (Edward had not forgotten either; on a recent occasion when they had had a ridiculous row and Gillian had got up on a very high horse indeed, Edward had the following day sent round to her flat a huge, stuffed, rather moth-eaten owl. It was still there, shedding dust and feathers on her books.)

She smoothed her hair, ready to go downstairs and face the day's adventures. The house was quiet, Bee and Toby having already left, but the sunshine outside was more inviting than the stale chill in the kitchen, and she carried her coffee to the garden at the back. Bee and Toby were not gardeners, Gillian had realized as soon as she had arrived the day before, but the four square yards of baked earth and scraggly foliage in front had not adequately prepared her for the larger area of neglect behind.

A high, rotting fence enclosed a wilderness of unpruned trees, broken bits of masonry and tangles of morning glory. A leggy rosebush put forth a few deformed blossoms of a morbid red. She opened the gate and looked into a dank, narrow walk, fenced on either side and presumably leading to Grantchester Street. It was muddy and weedy—a useful short cut for heavily laden shoppers, but hardly a walk to be taken for pleasure. She closed the gate again and went back to the patch of mangy turf close to the kitchen door. A round metal table, rust bubbling through its white paint, stood among several rickety garden chairs of which the birds had made frequent use. She would not be able to sit there unless she first scrubbed one of the seats. She returned to the pokey kitchen, leaving the door open while she drank her coffee and read *The Times*. Then she collected her key and locked up the house before setting off down Grantchester Meadows towards the heart of Cambridge.

She strolled up Grantchester Street, past the school and the post office and a small grocery shop, and came to Newnham Road beside Caius' playing field. The field was immaculate and empty, the nets and the players gone until spring. Beyond its flat, green expanse and pretty little pavilion marched a low hedge and some houses of brick in dull colours, and further away, she could just see the snub-nosed tip of the University Library tower, a plebeian erection that thrust itself, unwelcome, into many cherished views of Cambridge. She paid it little attention, however, being taken up with gazing at the solid Victorian brick and agreeable white trim of her own college. It loomed in the distance behind the playing field, looking both elaborate and cosy, like a well-to-do Dutch merchant's house.

Cosy it was not, Gillian remembered. An arctic atmosphere had prevailed in the corridors, producing what was known as 'the Newnham crouch'—a vain effort to minimize the loss of body heat by propelling oneself in a scuttling, hunched rush from one electric fire to the next. She had lived in college for a year before moving to small, equally frigid rooms of her own, from one window of which she could see the pinnacles of King's College chapel.

Not having lived long in Newnham, she retained an affection for it that was more attenuated than that of its undergraduates, for many of whom its rooms and corridors and quiet gardens were the irreplaceable vessels of their Cambridge memories. Still, Newnham was her college, she had dined in hall often and had read Proust lying under the hawthorn trees; she wanted it all to be there and not to have changed.

She walked along the edge of the playing field and then up Church Rate Walk. Little houses, a brick wall overhung with yew branches, it all looked the same. Then she turned the corner into Newnham Walk, and there at the end stood the high, brick gates of the college. There were Old Hall and Pfeiffer, and beyond lay Clough and Peile and the shade-dappled gardens. Her spirits rose: here was the Cambridge she knew. A moment later her pleasure in the remembered sustained a blow as the vista opened out and she saw a huge, new block of students' rooms on her right, where there had once been grass and trees. It wasn't a bad building, she supposed, and it certainly was nothing like as peculiar as the Principal's Lodge, but its diagonal placement fought with the geometry of the older structures. She turned back to the familiar façade of Old Hall, and as she stepped through the door into the cool, bare, white-painted interior, she felt that the essentials had remained. A little notice about students' milk loosed a flutter of memories: pasty-faced girls in wool dressing-gowns huddled over mugs of cocoa at dawn,

Caroline Fenwick in an astonishing negligée, brewing tea and reciting rude rhymes about her cast-off lovers, Bee, writing furiously—her table a litter of half-empty cups—and saying suddenly, 'I would rather be doing this than anything in the world.' She walked through into Pfeiffer to climb the handsome stairway with its graceful, arched white woodwork and bay windows looking east over the gates. Hearing the sound of voices coming from the top floor, she retreated and wandered into the gardens behind, where a peaceful expanse of lawn and pond and trees was surrounded by the earliest college buildings. This had not changed, it seemed to her, and she stood still, feeling a little ghostly, remembering summer afternoons long ago. She had come and gone, and Newnham had continued without her. Where she had once been a figure in the landscape, she was now invisible. After a while she turned away and drifted back down Newnham Walk, an elegiac mood seeping into her.

The mood held as she crossed Coe Fen, strolling past the cows grazing tranquilly on either side of the path. Golden leaves spattered the surface of the water below the Granta, where she had sat drinking beer on many a warm afternoon; the ducks were still there, swimming under the willows. On the other side of the fen, beyond the river, construction was going on; she could see cranes and scaffolding. She paid little attention, and she passed the University Centre with scarcely a glance, intent upon the intact pieces of her past. She passed over the foot-bridge, up the lane and across Silver Street, where the dark and sooty walls of Queens' frowned above the narrow pavement. The street was noisy, full of cars and bicycles and scurrying students, but as she turned the corner and entered the college gate, deep silence fell as if a heavy curtain had closed behind her. She crossed the first court to the far archway, going straight to Cloister Court near the river. Like the chapel at King's, this little court of fifteenth-century brick and Elizabethan half-timbering held a distillation of memory.

She walked in and expelled her breath in a relieved sigh. It was the same. Here time held still and inviolate, defended by ancient walls, drenched in reflective silence. This was a sanctuary, keeping at bay, or so she felt, all that was crude and false and violent. Long before, she had stood here and felt that to be a scholar was a splendid thing; this was a feeling that in the intervening years of mundane tasks and interruptions of tasks had become gradually submerged, but it flooded up from the depths now, a renewal of the spirit. As she retraced her steps between the perfect rectangles of green turf, she thought that what she would like to know was whether to live and work in Cambridge was to receive such a gift each day, or whether, even here, one would slip into indifference, going blindly through the daily round, to be startled into awareness only now and then by nature's rarer tricks—a fall of snow, or the brief flowering of a Judas-tree.

Armed against the hazards of the day, she spent the rest of the morning wandering through the city, up Botolph Lane with its terrace houses in ice-cream pastels, along Bene't Street, flaunting its apostrophe as if defying the erosion of time, and through the market, which was bigger and livelier than she remembered. Fading awnings sheltered fish and cheese and tattered Penguins, while banks of flowers made bright ramparts along the pavement. The stalls overflowed with autumn fruits and vegetables: greengages, scarlet runner beans, shiny courgettes, brilliant tomatoes from nearby farms, tiny baskets of berries, and boxes of rosy Cox's Orange Pippins and huge, misshapen Bramleys. Her eye lit upon a padded box of fat, purple figs. Seized by sudden greed, she bought three and carried them off to a sunny bench, where she ate them, one after another.

Above the market rose the solid edifice of Great St. Mary's, towering over the little bustling lives below as the grand geography of the colleges dwarfed the town. She did not climb the tower; she would do that later, she decided, wishing she could take Edward there. He had never visited Cambridge;

he was a Londoner and rarely left his city. Passing the church, she walked up narrow, book-lined Trinity Street towards the massive portals of Trinity College. They glowered over a short, bleak stretch of grey cobblestones, as though to discourage frivolous intrusion. Undaunted, she passed through into Great Court. Its sheer size was a shock after so long an absence. It was the enclosure, the privacy of such vastness that surprised, following the cramped streets without. The effect was precisely the opposite of that of public parks, which open the confinement of city streets to light and air. The huge court seemed to crush the little streets beside it, appropriating their sky to its own use. Nevertheless, the court itself was not overpowering. Its vast dimensions would have doubtless been endowed with a terrifying severity in France, but here the centuries unbent in a kindlier austerity and an English disregard for symmetry. Gillian stood in the middle of the court, not quite at home, thinking of Alistair Greenwood. She remembered—it was one of her sharpest images of Cambridge, though not sunlit—seeing him one late, blustery November day, crossing Trinity Great Court. The whole enormous space had been empty but for his solitary figure moving swiftly across it, intent, oblivious, his gown billowing in the Cambridge wind.

Gillian stayed a little while in Trinity, admiring the Wren library, and then wandered through the more intimate courts of Trinity Hall (where she had once reclined on a velvet sofa while a dazzling boy had recited John Donne as he removed her clothes) and Clare and then past her old rooms. She glanced up at the windows—her windows—but did not attempt to go in. She did not want to intrude upon some youthful stranger living there. And so at last she went to King's, the golden centre of her own Cambridge, where she had lain on the grass by the Cam on sunny afternoons, where she had fallen in love (if only for a little while), where she had learned so much of her craft under Basil Peters' tutelage, and where the chapel had shed its grace over the city.

She went through the college gate and gazed across the court at the chapel. It stood in isolated glory, turrets and pinnacles marching against the sky, rich, magniloquent, unrivalled. As if in a dream, she walked beside it and entered the great southern door. And inside was the cool silence she remembered, the still point of the turning world.

She stayed a long time, and then, feeling as though the entire sordid history of humanity had been redeemed, she eventually went out again and made her way back to Grantchester Meadows to ready herself for the afternoon's test of mettle.

CHAPTER 6

Gillian had been delighted to find that she was to give her lecture at King's. It was fortuitous, the meetings of the Cambridge Historical Society being held in turn at various colleges, but it seemed fitting that the formal occasion of her return to Cambridge should be held in the college that was the gatekeeper of her memories.

Dressing, that Monday afternoon, she felt confident, with just a pleasant edge of apprehension. But later, as she walked along King's Parade and through the college gates, her mood shifted. The turrets of the chapel rose above her, white gold against the sharp blue of the sky. She felt her confidence leaching away like sand sucked from beneath her feet by the sea. It was dangerous, this visionary Cambridge. The illusion gathered about her as swift and imperceptible as darkness or dawn: this is the centre, this is what matters, this is where you, the scholar, the supplicant, will be consecrated or cast out. She emerged from the court at the rear and looked towards the river. The green lawns of the Backs flowed away to infinity. The world, the years of work elsewhere—on some periphery—slid below the horizon.

She hurried on through the less intimidating confines of Webb Court and into King's Lane. She had never been in the Chetwynd Room before. She imagined what lay ahead: a room of some grandeur in scale and appointments, rows of formidable dons, grey as sharks, Greenwood's elegant introduction, a prelude that would dim the performance. And her lecture, no doubt sowing questions among the audience like dragon's teeth, each one to spring up afterwards a fully armed warrior, but not in her service. Her heart thumped, and she felt about as large and interesting as a pea.

She found Chetwynd Court, a drab and inconspicuous space squeezed between the lane and the opulent immensity of Great Court. Shut off from the lane by a palisade of high metal bars, it was a peculiar piece of joinery between Chetwynd Building, a handsome structure in Gothic style, its stones faintly golden like those of the chapel, and Keynes Building, a grey edifice of concrete and glass. The former, with its arched windows and parapet and carved angels, was linked to the latter by a short, recessed wall composed of enormous windows. Through them she could see a grand piano and some people drifting about. Nervousness gripped her; she wished she had not come.

She crossed the court to a massive, five-sided tower crowned with a rampart and a weathervane; beside its outsize, arched wooden door a little placard read 'Chetwynd Room.' Pushing open the heavy door, she found herself in a grand circular stairwell that spiralled above her past leaded-glass windows, and below her down into darkness. There were two doors on her level, one unlabelled, the other reading, unhelpfully, 'No Entrance.' She was wondering whether to go up the stairs or through the blank door, when a pudgy, bespectacled young man in a grimy sweater hurried past her through the door. She caught a glimpse of people and coathangers and followed him in.

Behind the door was a dismal little cloakroom with an acoustic tile ceiling and a strip of fluorescent lighting. No one paid her any attention, and she used the moment's respite to gather her courage. She could hear the clink of teacups and a low buzz of chatter. The door opened again and Greenwood appeared. He came straight over to her.

'You found it easily?' he inquired pleasantly. 'I'm sorry not to have accompanied you here, but I had something quite urgent to attend to just now. Allow me to take you in and give you some tea.' He led the way to another door on the right-hand side of the room; Gillian followed him through it. And came promptly down to earth.

The Chetwynd Room was far from what her imagination had conjured from her green and gold memories of King's. It was small, and ugly as only cheap modernity can be. Like the cloakroom, it rejoiced in fluorescent lighting and a ceiling of acoustic tiles. Its squat proportions fought with the arched windows of the gothic exterior, and institutional buff paint was chalky on the walls. Crowded into one side of the room were perhaps twenty people standing about, drinking tea. The remainder of the space was occupied by rows of black plastic chairs. They faced a small, slightly raised platform on which rested several more chairs and a battered table. At the back of the room was a large open hatch; tea was being served at the counter, in thick cafeteria cups. Nearby, a table offered a selection of anaemic sandwiches and small squares of cake. Young men and old men stood about, conversing in subdued tones. Gillian felt simultaneously relieved and annoyed. The roller-coaster had flattened out beneath her.

'I regret that the meeting is not being held at one of the other colleges, Emmanuel, for example,' said Greenwood, handing her a cup of tea. 'This room is rather unprepossessing. But then King's has a peculiar yearning to be modern. Perhaps that meets with your approval.'

'It meets with something more ambivalent,' Gillian replied. She was curious about what she saw here. Was it a deliberate attempt to dismantle the myth, to cast off privilege and be an extension of the ordinary world, rather than a separate kingdom? Or was it an accidental by-product of economy? And what would be left if a modern puritanical rage swept away all the splendid relics of the enfolding past?

More truth, or less conviction? She had no time to consider the question. Greenwood was making introductions.

Hugh Morecambe, whom she met first, was an historian at Peterhouse. He was tall and stoop-shouldered and balding and had a look of reptilian intelligence. His skin was creased and leathery, and this, together with the way his head poked forward as he extended his hand, made her think of a malevolent tortoise. He had been speaking to a younger man from the same college, whose name was Clive Barker, or possibly Parker. Barker-Parker was short and thin with dark hair, a fastidious little moustache and a prissy expression. Gillian was fascinated by his profile, which receded rapidly in all directions from his huge, sharp nose. Above his collar protruded a large and mobile Adam's apple; his skin looked pink and scraped, and he had an indefinable air of physical incompetence. Gillian thought that he probably nicked himself shaving nearly every time: she could see him wincing and pulling little dried-up tufts of Kleenex off his lacerated throat. Quelling these unkind irrelevancies, she made herself pay attention to the conversation. The gentle buzz of academic shop-talk surrounded them. Morecambe, learning that she was spending a sabbatical in London, asked her whether she made much use of the Reading Room at the British Museum, since by the time her next sabbatical came round, this reverenced institution would doubtless have been obliterated by the forces of progress. He told a long, quite funny story about hunting down a lost document, in the course of which he managed to let her know that he was intimately acquainted with the archives in Paris, Bonn, Lisbon and Madrid. He did it well. Barker-Parker then told a story about an Italian archivist who so resented the intrusions of scholars into his orderly domain that he instituted a system of perpetual recataloguing and actually managed to keep everyone out for almost four years. From there, the talk drifted to the deviant obsessions of archivists in general, their passion for order and its uneasy intercourse with the scholar's passion for search. It was articulate fluff of the sort at which the English excelled; it kept everyone amused and at a comfortable distance from each other. Gillian thought: *No Content Please, We're British.*

After a few minutes she escaped, having seen an old and cherished acquaintance helping himself to some tea. This was Basil Peters, her thesis supervisor. She made her way over to him, glad to see someone she both liked and admired. The intervening years had changed him only a little; he was stouter, his hair was grizzled, and the skin beneath his eyes was pouchy, but he looked pink-cheeked and wide awake, as if he had just been for a country walk, and she recognized the old quizzical glance and warm smile.

'Gillian. Welcome back to Cambridge. What's taken you so long?'

'Basil. What a pleasant sight you are. Now that I see you, I can't imagine what's kept me away.'

He grasped her hand with the warmth of an embrace. 'How long are you staying? Can you come to dinner tomorrow? Elizabeth would be delighted to see you, too.'

'There's nothing I'd rather do. Do you still make that extraordinary Jamaican punch? I have a feeling I'll need some after this ordeal.'

He gave her a sly smile. 'Trial by Oxbridge? Don't worry, Gillian. We've grown old and toothless since your oral.'

'Toothless? This room is full of piranha fish. And Greenwood is a shark—the man-eating sort.'

Basil laughed. 'Bite him back, that's my advice. Nobody does any more. I expect he pines for a little thrust and parry. And now, tell me what you have been doing lately. I saw your book on settlers and civil servants; I thought it was excellent—gave it to one of my students who's writing a thesis on decolonization in the Caribbean. He's an interesting fellow; he should be here. I'd like to introduce you to him.'

Gillian talked for a few minutes about the work she was doing in London. '...I look like a coal miner by the end of the day—smudges of newsprint all over me. And cultural change is so amorphous, it's hard to know how to dissect it. At least this talk I'm giving today is partly about something concrete: what was actually written in the newspapers on the subject of empire. But trying to define the relationship between what was written and what people's attitudes to the empire actually were is like trying to walk across a bog. I may sink out of sight very quickly.' She asked Basil about his work; he had been in Jamaica and Grenada in the spring.

A few late-comers arrived; the room began to feel crowded. Basil said: 'You've drawn a respectable throng, I see. You probably don't know any of the younger men, but there must be quite a few familiar faces. I didn't realize that you knew Morecambe.'

'I don't. Greenwood introduced us. He's a malicious bugger, isn't he? Greenwood, I mean. He knew perfectly well that we wouldn't connect. What I don't understand is why they're here at all.'

'People generally do attend when the subject is of interest to them. Morecambe, and Barker for that matter, will probably be more surprised than you will like if you give an interesting lecture—and I don't doubt that you will—but they won't be so encased in their prejudices as to be incapable of appreciating it. They're not as bad as you think.'

Gillian sighed. 'Basil, I should come and be your student again. You could give me lessons in humanity. There's something about this place that acidulates the mind—but not yours.'

'Oh, I'm merely growing old, my dear. I haven't the energy to be indignant.'

Gillian was reminded of a question she had wanted to ask Basil years earlier but had never come near asking because it was personal. Had he ever been jealous of Greenwood's public glory? Basil Peters was as great an historian as Alistair Greenwood, but no one outside the world of scholarship and letters knew who he was, whereas Greenwood's flamboyance, his aura of The Great Man, had attracted a far wider audience. Basil was not the kind of small man who would simply reverse his snobbery accordingly, but had he ever yearned for equal recognition? Now was not the time to ask—she probably never would ask—nevertheless, it was interesting that people were not jealous of Basil's achievements as they were undeniably jealous of Greenwood's.

Just then Basil, who was facing the doorway, said, 'Here comes my student.' Gillian turned and saw something unexpected: a tall, handsome, quite black young man. He came over to them with a fluid, unhurried stride.

'Gillian, I'd like you to meet Jon Hay.' She was thinking: Oh my, how delicious—and he probably thinks I look like a hospital matron in these conservative clothes—oh well.

Hay had a deep, expressive voice and an engagingly cocky manner. He was well aware of his attractions and turned them full on for Gillian's benefit. While she enjoyed this, she was not drawn in; she was pretty sure he would have done the same had she been afflicted with three chins and dowager's hump. Nor did it prevent a reasonable exchange of views about the problems of writing colonial history, it simply went on automatically, like a solar-activated bulb. Gillian was irrationally comforted by Hay's presence; she had been feeling like the only strawberry in a cucumber patch, and now at least there was a lone aubergine.

A few moments later, Greenwood approached her, the crowd seeming to part for him like the Red Sea, and suggested that it was time that they proceed with the meeting. She followed him to the platform, and they sat down at the table. The audience shuffled towards the plastic chairs, the older members occupying the seats at the front. Rows of faces seamed with age, bodies bent and crabbed with disuse, bald heads, liver spots, and myopia confronted Gillian. Dressed like scarecrows, but clothed in wisdom, the venerable historians of Cambridge awaited her words.

Gillian herself had prepared her appearance with care, hoping to look more formidable than she felt. Her skirt was rather long, to avoid offering any unseemly glimpses of thigh, her jacket was of a severe cut and dark colour. Should she sweat, no one would know. She wore no jewellery except a pair of discreet gold earrings, her scarf was a virginal white, and her scent would barely have been noticed by a serious gathering of wine-tasters. She had laughed about this with Bee when she had dressed earlier that day. 'Why do I think I should masquerade as a nun? Is celibacy the mark of true scholarship?'

'Ask your friend Greenwood,' Bee had replied.

She put her cards and papers in a tidy pile on the table in front of her and crossed her legs. Her nervousness returned. In the back of the room, behind the fierce old men, were scattered the seeds of the coming generation: young men, hirsute and untidy, soon to be bald and untidy. Did something about the academic life hasten the loss of hair, she wondered. A couple of women came in late and sat off to one side, looking her over with curiosity. At the rear, while the final stragglers drifted towards their chairs, the teacups were being noisily cleared away. When the last of them had been pushed across the counter, a metal blind came down with a grating rattle. It did not quite close, and the sound of crockery being stacked could still be heard.

Then the door opened again and closed, and two more people came in. To Gillian's utter surprise, and mixed consternation and pleasure, one of them was Edward. He met her eyes discreetly and found himself an empty chair in the back row. He hadn't told her he was coming; he must have extricated himself from his work at the last moment and driven up from London. Among the baggy, rumpled, abstracted academics, Edward was an arresting sight. His clothes were impeccable, if conventional, and they fitted his lithe, compact, athlete's body. He had dark hair, as dense and shining as the coat of a Burmese cat, deep-set eyes and thick, dark brows. His nose was thin and slightly curved, with no flesh on it, his mouth well defined, disciplined, but quick with a vivid sense of the absurd. Perhaps because she was seeing him unexpectedly—or perhaps it was the setting—Gillian saw him again as she had the afternoon they had met, two years before. Then, she could not define what she saw. Now she identified it, although she was dissatisfied with her words. It was immediacy: a concentrated energy poured into the present moment that charged it with intensity. Around him, the other faces looked half-alive, their intensity remote and inward. Seeing him suddenly in that ugly little room among the collocation of academic men, she felt a wave of longing wash through her and briefly imagined standing up and walking out of the door, walking away with him, anywhere. Then reality reclaimed her: Greenwood had begun to speak.

The minutes of the previous meeting were disposed of with informal brevity, then he introduced her to her audience. He was not elaborate; the setting, or the occasion, was unworthy, Gillian guessed. He referred to her Cambridge degree and her present position, sketched her previous work in British imperial history, and read out the title of her paper. That was the worst moment. As she stood up, opened her mouth, and the first words of her lecture somehow issued forth, she relaxed. This was nothing new and impossible, she had done it before, over and over again. She talked, they listened. She referred to the notes on her little cards now and then. She forgot the teacups and had no idea when the sounds ceased. Time passed, and, miraculously, she had spoken for half an hour, and she was finished.

The audience applauded. It sounded more than polite. Gillian, smiling a little, stood a few feet from Greenwood's chair, feeling a profound relief that it was over. It was quite dark outside, she noticed. The questions were still to come, of course, but she felt ready.

The applause sounded loud in the bare room. Edward was clapping and looking at her with something like proprietary pleasure. Suddenly there was a louder noise, and she was simultaneously aware of a movement to her left and a gasp from the audience. She turned; Greenwood had fallen sideways off his chair. He was sprawled over the edge of the platform, his hand at his chest. Gillian's first thought was: My God, he's had a heart attack. She darted across to him. His face was grey. But if his heart had stopped, it had not stopped of its own accord. Blood spread around his hand. The hand moved convulsively, and Gillian saw a hole. More blood welled out of it. Instinctively, she glanced towards the back of the room. The door was closed. She saw Edward vaulting over his chair.

Pandemonium had broken out in the audience. Men were standing up and shouting. Chairs scraped on the floor as some of them tried to struggle past others who were standing still craning their necks. Those at the front saw the blood and cried out in shock. Some further back remained seated, bewildered by the sudden violent confusion. Blood kept spreading over Greenwood's chest. Basil, who had been sitting in the front row, reached the body first; he pressed his handkerchief over the wound. People crowded round, then someone shouted that Greenwood needed air and tried to push them back. Gillian knelt too, the chaos loud in her ears. She made a pad of her white scarf and handed it to Basil, who placed it over his soaked handkerchief. Its whiteness was immediately stained with brilliant scarlet, and an image from long ago flashed through Gillian's mind: blood on the snow in the field behind her house, great drops of it between the hoof prints of a wounded stag the hunters had not followed. Christ almighty, she thought. He's been shot, he's been shot. And I didn't recognize the sound through the applause.

Then, over the tumult, she heard a familiar voice. 'Let me through. I'm a police officer.' Edward scythed through the pack and came to her side. Gillian's scarf was already saturated, and Edward, imperious in emergency, demanded and received handkerchiefs and a cravat from the nearest members of the crowd. Basil took them with bloody fingers. 'Who knows where the nearest telephone is?' asked Edward brusquely. Several voices responded. He chose someone Gillian could not see. 'Send for an ambulance and report back immediately. Please,' he added, but it was not a request.

Meanwhile, Gillian had gathered her wits. Artificial respiration, she thought and pulled Greenwood's head back, pinching his nose with her left hand. Four quick breaths and then fifteen a minute, I think. She hoped she was doing it correctly; she hadn't had to use it since she had learned how. Edward glanced down, left her to it, and commandeered an anorak to tie around the wad of handkerchiefs on Greenwood's chest. Then he faced about, standing on the platform above the press, and took control. 'Stand back, please. I am Detective Chief Inspector Gisborne of Scotland Yard.' The crowd receded a little and the noise died down. 'I must request all of you to return to your seats and remain there until an officer of the Cambridge police arrives.' Several voices began asking questions; no one sat down. All Gillian could see when her eyes left Greenwood's chest was Edward's back and Basil's worried face bending over the body. Beyond was a dark, restless forest of trouser legs. Then, from somewhere behind the crowd, a high voice called out, 'I've rung for an ambulance.'

'Good,' said Edward. 'Then ring the police. They'll come in any case, but I'd like you to tell them Professor Greenwood has been shot and that an officer from Scotland Yard is here and will take charge until they arrive.'

'Yes. All right,' Gillian heard, and then Edward raised his voice a little more. 'The rest of you gentlemen, please sit down now. As you will readily understand, it is necessary to clear the way for the stretcher and minimize the disturbance in the room.' This calculated appeal to the audience's intelligent grasp of essentials was effective. The men retreated to their chairs. The room became quieter. 'Thank you,' Edward said. 'Please remain where you are.' A siren could be heard coming closer. Heads turned towards the door. Edward looked back at Gillian. 'Is he breathing at all?'

'Don't think so,' Gillian said briefly, between breaths.

'Keep at it anyhow.'

She had a clear view to the back of the room now. A quick thunder of footsteps was heard outside the door. A voice called, 'In here,' and two men with a stretcher ran in, followed by a pale, thin young man, his clothing flapping about his twig-like limbs. One of the men knelt down by Greenwood's side and examined him. There was no breath, no heart-beat. The blood had stopped flowing and was turning dark at the edges of the stains. The man turned Greenwood's head a little, and Gillian looked into lifeless eyes. Edward stood over the ambulance attendant, who looked up and said, 'How long?'

'About eight minutes ago.'

'He's dead, I'm afraid. There's nothing we can do now.'

Edward's response was unhesitating. 'Then don't move him. Can you wait outside a moment? The police should be here immediately.'

The audience sat frozen while the stretcher-bearers hurried out of the room. Then they began talking again in low, shocked tones. Gillian stood up and quickly sat down again, feeling dizzy and nauseated and wishing for a stiff belt of brandy. Basil, looking old and weary, leaned on the table, while Edward stood guard over the room, arms folded, facing the door. Time hung still in a dreadful, endless moment of inactivity. Then, in the murmurous hush, a plaintive voice rose from the back row. An ancient, cadaverous man with rheumy, half-blind eyes and the petrified remains of some long-forgotten meal clinging to his tie, got to his feet and said in faintly querulous tones, 'Could someone please tell me what is going on? If time permits, I should like to ask Dr. Adams—'

Then the police arrived.

CHAPTER 7

The policemen rushed through the door; suddenly the room seemed to be full of them, surging around the immobilized academics like water rushing across a cellar floor. Several of them went into a quick huddle with Edward, over by the window, while Gillian, who had had enough of being conspicuous, left the platform and sat with Basil among her former audience. The academics muttered among themselves, glancing uneasily at the knot of policemen by the window. They were wondering what would happen next, and what they were supposed to do. Some looked covertly at their watches. They had other commitments, no doubt—wives or students waiting, or meetings to attend—and they hardly knew whether they would be leaving soon, or whether to telephone, or even whether it was acceptable to be thinking of such mundane matters at this moment. Gillian glanced at her own watch. It was only 5:30.

The mills of the law began to grind. More policemen arrived. One remained by the door, while others went out again, presumably to search the building and the surrounding courts. After some minutes, during which the restless anxiety of the sequestered crowd became palpable, one policeman detached himself from the group at the window and walked to the front of the room. He stood on the platform, his large body screening Greenwood's corpse and the two other policemen who were examining it. As he loomed up before her, Gillian was suddenly struck by the thought that he did not look out of place in the room; he and the other policemen were natural inhabitants of its utilitarian space, more at home than the historians gathered there.

He said: 'I am Detective Chief Superintendent Hardy. I am afraid I must inform you that Professor Alistair Greenwood is dead.' He paused while his audience absorbed the blow. They had known it, of course, but the bald announcement sealed the fact, made it irreversible. He continued: 'It is my duty to take charge of the investigation, and you will understand that the necessary procedures may result in some inconvenience to yourselves. We shall do our best to minimize it. Each of you will be interviewed as soon as time allows; meanwhile, you will kindly identify yourselves to Detective-Constable Petrie.' His eyes swept over them. 'Did anyone see who shot Professor Greenwood?' No one spoke. 'Very well. Can anyone suggest a nearby room where all of you might be able to wait more comfortably?' (And not be underfoot, Gillian added silently.)

Cecil Corbett, a Tudor historian at King's, answered him. 'It may seem inappropriate, but I think perhaps the bar is the simplest solution. It's just along the passage.' This idea was accepted, and the corpus of academics was escorted out discreetly, leaving the room to another profession. Gillian went too, giving her name and Bee's address to the detective at the door before passing through it, followed by Basil.

In the bar, she was glad of her position as woman and guest. She was one of the first to obtain a drink, and she felt ready for several. The men huddled at the bar, talking in spectral whispers. A few students who had been sitting in the comfortable chairs scattered about, chatting amicably, stared with unconcealed curiosity at the invasion of historians and their accompanying police officer. Gillian gazed round the room, which was full of blond wood and reminded her unpleasingly of California, and found a soft chair. She sank into it and closed her eyes but, seeing the image of Greenwood's body, quickly opened them again. She drank her whisky and was glad to see Basil bringing her another. He sat down next to her.

'Earth, receive an honoured guest,' Gillian said sadly, and they drank together in silence.

After a lengthy wait in the bar, during which a fitful, shambling parade of hunched, miserable, subdued academics was put with exemplary gentleness and efficiency through the detectives' sieve, Edward at last appeared.

'Sorry I've been so long. How are you bearing up?'

'I'm surviving.'

'Good,' Edward said briefly. He was not exactly perfunctory, but his mind was on the dead, not the living. 'Look. I've been asked to stay on and help. Cutter—the Divisional Chief Superintendent—knows me. It will have to be cleared at the Yard, but as I was on the spot when Greenwood was shot, it's hardly likely that the request will be denied. I don't know where I'll be staying; Cutter will arrange something...'

Gillian nodded. 'Of course. But Edward, what happened? Where did the shot come from?'

'Greenwood was shot by someone standing in the little scullery behind the Chetwynd Room. The metal blind wasn't fully closed; it would have been easy to aim a pistol through the crack at the bottom—the track is slightly bent and kept the blind from closing properly, but whether by accident or design we don't know. The noise was noticeable, of course, and recognizable to me, but the applause obscured its direction, and the panic gave him time to get away.'

'Him? Did you see him?'

'No. Whoever it was made a damned quick exit. By the time I opened the door, no one was there.'

'Which way do you think he went?' asked Basil. 'There are three ways out.'

'Three?' said Gillian.

'Out through the courtyard, up the stairs, and along the corridor to the bar,' said Edward. 'He's certain to have gone outside, he would have been seen in the bar, and though there's no one about upstairs at the moment the risk of being seen there would have been worse than the risk in the courtyard.'

'Did no one see him?' asked Basil. 'The bar overlooks the court.'

'It's dark outside,' Edward replied. 'And I didn't know the layout, so I hesitated.'

Gillian spoke up. 'What were you doing here, anyway? You appeared like a genie out of a bottle.'

'I came up to hear your lecture. And to stay over until tomorrow. I didn't know I was going to be able to get away until I found myself walking out of the door. I tried to ring the number you gave me, but no one answered. You're still staying there?'

'Yes. I had thought of going back to London tomorrow, but as it is...' She trailed off uncertainly.

'You'll probably be free to leave as soon as you've given a statement to the police, but I hope you'll hang on for a little while. It probably won't take long to clear this up, and then we could drive back together.' He began to move away.

'Edward!' Gillian said urgently. 'I have something to tell you.'

'What is it?'

'Greenwood was almost shot yesterday—at lunch.'

'What?' Edward's yelp of astonishment was echoed by Basil. Heads turned in their direction.

'A girl was there, she had a gun and while we were all eating lunch she pulled it out and aimed it at Greenwood. Pamela Ditton—his cousin—grabbed her arm and the bullet went into the wall,' Gillian said as rapidly and quietly as she could.

'What girl? What was her name?'

'Fiona Clay.'

'Where did this happen?'

'At Greenwood's house, in Little Camford.'

'What became of the gun? Where is it? Did he tell the police?' The questions came like machine-gun fire.

'No. And he kept the gun himself.'

'He did? What the devil did he do that for?'

'I don't know.'

'Good God. Well, you'll obviously have to tell me the whole story. Wait here for a minute while I have a word with Hardy.' He hurried out of the room.

'Why did she try to shoot him?' Basil asked.

'I'm not sure. I'm sorry, but I think I probably shouldn't say anything about it until Edward comes back.'

Basil raised his eyebrows. 'Detective Chief Inspector—er—Gisborne, was it? seems to have a remarkable facility for being in the right place at the right time. Do murders usually happen under his nose? You seem to be rather matey with him, old girl.'

Gillian turned pink, but she said stoutly, 'Yes. I am.'

'How extraordinary,' Basil said, amused. 'Bring him along to dinner tomorrow if he's able to come.'

'Thank you, Basil. You are kind.'

'Not at all. I'm burning with curiosity.'

'He'll probably be too much in the thick of the investigation, but I'll try.'

Edward came back. 'It's arranged. I want to hear all about this bizarre lunch of yours, preferably while we're having a bite ourselves. I've eaten nothing since early this morning. You'll have to give Hardy a synopsis and a description first; he'll want to search for the girl right away.'

The other people in the room were watching them avidly.

'All right. Just let me introduce you to Professor Basil Peters, my friend and former thesis adviser. Basil, this is Edward Gisborne.' The two men shook hands, and Basil, with tact and charm, invited Edward to dinner. Edward, as Gillian had expected, said only that he would be delighted to come if he could. She followed him out and waited in the horrible little cloakroom while Edward went into the Chetwynd Room to fetch Hardy. She caught a glimpse of lights and boxes of equipment and realized that the police photographers must be at their grisly task.

Edward came out again promptly, accompanied by the tall, heavy-bodied, blue-eyed man who had taken charge before she and the others had been herded off to the bar. She gave him a bald account of the events at Greenwood's house and a vivid description of Fiona Clay which she then qualified: 'But if she doesn't look like that all the time, then I can't help you much, I'm afraid. She could look like anything at all, in ordinary garb.'

Hardy eyed her a moment. 'Minus the costume, she's twenty, five foot eight or nine, dark hair, white skin, violet eyes. Violet?'

Gillian nodded. 'They were, really.'

Hardy and Edward conferred briefly; it was settled that Edward would bring Gillian to the police station later to make a full statement. She and Edward left the building, passed through the dim court beneath the banks of lighted windows in Keynes Building, and in a moment or two were slipping up the narrow lane towards King's Parade. Gillian felt a guilty sense of relief at her escape.

'Where shall we go?' asked Edward.

'What about a pub, or a wine bar?'

'Yes. Something quick and dirty.'

'There's a wine bar across the road. They do cold roast beef, salads, that sort of thing.'

'Fine. And afterwards, I'd like you to come with me to Greenwood's house. When I see it, I'll probably have some questions to ask you.'

'Yes, I'll come.' Gillian led him through a glass door, and they went down a spiral staircase into a plain, whitewashed room below street level. Edward inspected the decor. 'Less is more is an overrated theory,' he commented.

'At least there aren't any plants,' Gillian replied. 'I do get so sick of peering at people through the fronds of the fern bars.'

They collected some roast beef and some red wine. Edward tasted his. 'Not bad. I like drinking wine, but I don't see why I have to pretend I'm in some Mediterranean peasant's cellar in order to enjoy myself.'

'Oh, you Englishmen. You loathe everything foreign.'

'Not at all. You're foreign, for one thing.'

'Not very, you must admit.'

'I admit nothing. You are foreign. I must see if you haven't got it printed on you somewhere, like those odd bits of old pottery.'

'I may be odd, and even quite old, but I'll thank you not to be rude about it. Englishmen are supposed to be exquisitely polite, you know. It makes up for their reputed deficiencies.'

'Such as?'

Gillian smiled. 'Such as being arrogant and rotten in bed. In case you don't know it, English lovers bask in the same international reputation as English food.'

'Oh my God. Stop. Next time I'll be wondering whether I remind you of boiled cabbage.'

They drank some wine companionably and attacked the beef. 'Tell me about Fiona Clay,' Edward said. He listened attentively, interrupting only to ask an occasional question and once to say, 'You're a good witness, Gillian.' Gillian's spirits, which had lifted briefly in his company, sank again as she talked about Greenwood. She felt sombre and angry and bewildered. Edward's reaction remained invisible. 'That's a damned odd story, Gillian,' was all he said at the end. They did not linger over their meal.

Afterwards, moving along the dark roads in the car, Gillian shrank from going back to Greenwood's house. Noticing her discomfort, Edward put his hand briefly over hers as they slowed and turned in at the open gates. 'Buck up,' he murmured. They drove through deeper darkness under the trees and stopped near the end of the drive. Moonlight bleached the lawn to a dead grey. The house loomed up, a tall, black shape. They walked round to the front door where a constable was already in place, guarding the empty house from the intrusions of the curious. He unlocked the door for them and gave Edward a bunch of keys.

A table lamp lit the large hall; the other rooms were shrouded in darkness. Gillian felt like a thief, an invader. Alistair Greenwood had died and could no longer keep the world out of his hermitage. She and Edward, two strangers and two citizens of the modern world, were alien and unwelcome intruders. She imagined the house resisting them, doors sticking, beams falling on their heads, lights going out. Nothing happened. The house was wrapped in stillness.

'Show me the dining-room,' Edward said, his voice matter-of-fact. Had Gillian spoken first, she would have whispered. He followed her through the doorway. She groped and found a switch, and the sconces shed their subdued amber light over the silent room. On the sideboard, the silver tea service glittered against the dark wood as if lit for a Renaissance still life. 'What a beautiful room,' Edward said with quick pleasure. Then the policeman took over. 'Not enough light to see a damned thing.' He dug a torch out of his pocket. Its powerful beam flashed into the room, splitting it into random segments of livid brilliance. Light swept over polished surfaces, carved legs, handles, candlesticks, switches, windowpanes. The Renaissance tableau vanished, replaced by a cubist vision of disunited elements.

Edward inspected the wall where the bullet had been. 'A good thing she didn't hit that picture,' he remarked, taking a moment to admire it. 'Where was she sitting?'

'Here, next to Denham Greenwood.'

'And the rest of you?'

Gillian showed him. He fished a tape-measure out of his pocket and busied himself with a rough calculation of angle and distance. 'Here. Hold this end.' He glanced at his watch.

'Eight o'clock. Denham will hear from the police at any time now, I expect. I hope he can tell us where Fiona Clay is.' With Gillian's help, he reconstructed Fiona's and Pamela's actions. 'Pamela took rather a large risk.'

'She's used to guns. And she said she thought Fiona might put a hole in the Stubbs.'

Edward looked sardonic. 'A hole in Cousin Greenwood was preferable, I suppose.' He went to the sideboard, asking, 'Where did Greenwood put the gun?' Gillian pointed at the lower right-hand door, and Edward opened it, holding a small section of the handle in his handkerchief. His hand hovered over the three small drawers. 'Which one?' he asked. 'That one there,' she replied and he tugged at the middle drawer. It was locked. 'Mph,' he grunted. 'And what did you say Greenwood did with the key?'

'He put it on the key-ring in his pocket. I'm sure of that.'

'All right. Let's see what we have here.' Edward pulled a large ring of keys out of his coat pocket and spread it on his palm.

'Where did you get those?'

'From the constable. You saw him give them to me.'

'Yes, I know, but where did he get them?'

'From Hardy. They were in Greenwood's pocket.'

'Oh.' Gillian looked at them. Among the large, old-fashioned keys and the smaller modern ones, was a tiny, ornate, golden key. 'That looks like the one he used,' she said cautiously. 'I didn't have a close look at it.'

Edward sat on his heels and, using his handkerchief again, inserted the key into the lock of the middle drawer. He turned it gently; Gillian held her breath. Carefully, Edward pulled the drawer open, a little way at first, and then further. They peered into the long, shallow recess. It was empty.

'It's gone,' they said together. Then Gillian added, 'I'm not surprised.'

'Neither am I. I doubt very much that two different guns were pointed at Alistair Greenwood in the last two days. But who took the gun? And how did he open the drawer, I'd like to know. Come here, Gillian.'

She knelt down beside him. He shone the strong light of the torch on the polished surfaces of the sideboard. He closed the drawer and shone the torch at it from different angles, then he opened it slightly, and they scrutinized the top edge. 'Aren't you going to look for fingerprints?' Gillian asked.

'The lab will do that. Anyhow, no one leaves prints these days. I'm looking for something harder to remove.' He aimed the torch's beam sideways along the top surface of the drawer front, and then lay on his back and did the same to the bottom. 'There are no marks of force on this drawer that I can see. And if anyone had pried it open, no matter how carefully, wood this fine and polished would show it.' He closed the drawer again. 'So what did our gunman do?'

'Or gunwoman,' Gillian objected.

'It seems,' Edward continued smoothly, 'that the gunperson obtained the key.'

'But it's still on his key-ring, Holmes.'

'Don't be mundane. Possibly there's a duplicate key, obtained through a clever ruse by our master criminal.'

'Maybe Greenwood moved the gun himself.'

'Maybe he did, but that's a theory that cries out to be ignored. Where does it get us? If he moved the gun, he did so in order to destroy it—which he didn't do because we're assuming he was shot with it—or to use it, which he didn't. At least, no other bodies have turned up yet. Or he put it in a safer place, in which case we're back to the locked drawer again, except that we don't know where it is.'

'Stop. Stop. You've convinced me. Somebody managed to get a key. But how? And when?'

'I don't know yet.'

'Well,' said Gillian, frowning, 'he put the key in his pocket yesterday, and he had it in his pocket this afternoon. His house keys are on the ring—'

'And his car keys.'

'—So he wouldn't have left the house without them. I can't believe that anyone literally picked his pocket; therefore someone either burgled his house last night when he was asleep, or he left the keys in a coat or whatever while he was at the university today, and someone burgled his rooms.'

'In time to come out here for the gun and then return Greenwood's keys before he met you at the Chetwynd Room. How long would that take?'

'Assuming no difficulties with parking, about fifteen minutes each way. It all sounds quite improbable, doesn't it?'

'Yes. It's awkward. But if we eliminate the improbable, we're left with the impossible.'

They stared at the massive, finely made sideboard. 'What about the other drawers?' asked Gillian.

'Yes. I'd like to know what's in them, and where their keys are.'

'They weren't in their locks yesterday,' she said positively.

Handkerchief in hand, Edward tugged at the handles of the drawers above and below the central drawer which had held the gun. They were locked too. Then he began systematically and quickly opening and closing other doors and drawers. Port and madeira in crystal decanters, a silver box lined with cedar that smelt richly of cigars, snowy napery and polished glasses were stored in orderly reticence. He slid his hands beneath the folded squares of linen but found nothing. In another drawer, lined with felt, lay four mighty silver serving spoons. Gillian picked one up, coveting its weighty elegance, and turned it over to examine the marks. 'Who is Greenwood's heir?' she asked.

'We don't know yet. We'll hear something from his solicitor tomorrow.' Edward took the spoon from her and hefted it. 'How old is it?'

'George I or II, I'm not sure which. Aren't they splendid? And not locked up, which makes me even more curious about what's in the drawers that are locked.'

Edward put the spoon back in its drawer, running his fingers over the felt bottom. They encountered a small, flattish bump. 'What have we here, I wonder.' He lifted a corner of the lining, and one spoon slid against another. Under the felt, side by side, lay two tiny keys, each an apparent twin of the key that had opened the middle drawer. 'Well, well,' said Edward in pleased tones. He scooped up the keys, and, kneeling on the rug, inserted one into the lock of the middle drawer. It would not turn. Gillian squatted down beside him. 'Try the other one,' she said, as Edward was doing so. It would not turn either.

'So whoever it was didn't use one of these two keys to open that drawer,' Edward said. 'Now let's see what's in the others.' He tried the second key in the bottom drawer, and it turned smoothly. He pulled the drawer open. Inside was a shallow leather box, about twelve inches long. Gillian watched, riveted, as he took the box from the drawer and opened it. The box was lined in white satin, and nestled inside were a dozen silver teaspoons.

'Oh,' said Gillian, let down. 'Those are beautiful teaspoons, but somehow I expected something more significant.'

Edward laughed. 'A lost will, perhaps? If you expect to detect things whenever you're a detective, you'll frequently be disappointed.' He closed the drawer and locked it again with the spoons inside. Then he inserted the other key into the lock of the top drawer. It turned, the drawer opened. Another leather box lay within. 'Ho hum,' said Edward to Gillian and opened the box. A pretty array of mustard and salt spoons, sugar tongs and a marrow scoop met their eyes.

'That's that, then.' Edward snapped the box closed and put it back. 'Now. What about this house? I feel certain that no great skill would be required to enter it surreptitiously. Suppose the murderer came last night. What would he—he-or-she, that is—have tried first?'

'There are three doors to the outside, at least, but Greenwood must have locked them at night, especially last night.'

'We'll discover that the murderer overcame that small difficulty. He-or-she is undeterred by locks.'

'Edward. If we are going to carry on with this formal inquiry, I should like, while praising your fair-minded terminology, to point out that I cannot go on saying he-or-she every other sentence. Can't we call him-or-her X?'

'I'm bored with X. They're always called X.'

'I see. Is there some other letter of the alphabet that has recently struck your fancy?'

'No. That's why I keep saying he-or-she.'

Gillian snorted. 'No it isn't. You keep saying that to annoy me.'

'How true.'

'Well, come on. How about an acronym?'

'Why, yes, of course. If you like. Person Who Took Gun. PWTG,' said Edward, making a noise like a man with an extremely bad cold saying 'pudding.'

Gillian giggled helplessly. 'You fool.'

They were both sitting on the floor laughing indecorously when the constable poked his head round the door. 'You're wanted on the telephone, sir,' he said stiffly. He eyed Gillian with reproof, as though her presence were to blame for this unseemly frivolity, as indeed it was.

Oh dear, thought Gillian. He's right. We shouldn't be laughing. But Edward makes me laugh even in the midst of death and destruction. Edward got up. He had become the complete policeman again. As he followed the constable out of the room, Gillian got up too, brushing her skirt absentmindedly. Why didn't we hear the telephone, she wondered. Where was it? She supposed Greenwood had hated the infernal instrument and had relegated it to some obscure and unpleasant corner.

In a few minutes, Edward came back alone. 'That was the Superintendent. I've got to get back. First let's take a quick look at the library and the general layout of the house.'

Edward marched swiftly through the still, tenebrous rooms and passages, flashing his torch, switching lights on and off.

There were four large rooms on the main floor, apart from the hall and the kitchens in the rear. These were the morning-room and the library at the south end, and the enormous drawing-room and the dining-room at the opposite end. A broad staircase ran up into darkness, to a shadowy landing and a tall, uncurtained window, black against the night. There was a bathroom near the staircase, and a tiny, spartan telephone room had been built by subdividing an outsize closet off the main entrance. Behind the dining-room, the kitchens occupied the older part of the house. The ceilings were lower and the stone floors worn and uneven. The main kitchen and its subsidiary scullery and storage rooms were all clean, old-fashioned and functional. No attempt had been made at warmth or comfort; the Elizabethan cottage was not an Elizabeth David kitchen, but a place for hired help to work in.

In the bare little scullery at the end of the house were two huge sinks and a long table. A door opened directly into the kitchen garden; vegetables and fruit were brought in and cleaned here, keeping muck and unwanted foliage out of the storerooms and kitchen. Edward turned on the tap, and a furious rush of water thundered into the sink. 'Quite deafening,' he observed.

He finished his tour with despatch, reserving his inspection of the library until the end and pausing only to examine with care each door to the outside. 'Four doors,' he said at last. 'All open yesterday, no doubt, and none with a lock worth tuppence anyway. A trusting soul, one might conclude.'

'He was hardly that. He merely lived in the country.'

'Let's go upstairs for a moment.' Edward ran lightly up the wide steps, but Gillian lingered at the bottom, her eye caught by the newel-post, which was surmounted by a lion couchant. It was a splendid piece of carving and almost the only bit of frivolous ornamentation incorporated into the structure of the house. A builder's whim, or had it been added later? It was delightful, and its unexpected presence in those plain surroundings reminded Gillian of Greenwood's prose, which was in the main austerely elegant but always capable of surprising one with a deftly placed gracenote. She trailed up the stairs, disconsolate.

Edward said, 'There's nothing obvious to see up here. His bedroom is undisturbed, and the others appear to be unused. The Cambridge police can make a proper job of going through them.'

Gillian glanced briefly into Greenwood's bedroom. It was very large, cold and bare, with no hint of self-indulgence except the ornate headboard of the big bed and a charming Cotman watercolour. 'Let's go down to the library,' Edward said, turning away.

The door to the library was closed but not locked. Edward flung it wide and stepped briskly over the threshold. Inside, a faint smell of books infused the darkness. Shafts of moonlight slanted across the floor, casting a feeble grey light over the lowest tiers. This was the heart of Greenwood's citadel, and it was empty now.

Edward switched on the lights and strolled about, scanning the shelves cursorily. 'A marvellous collection—was he really a great historian, or was he just famous?'

'He was a very great historian,' Gillian said sadly. 'He had all this breadth—' she swept her arm out towards the silent books—'and the power of distillation. He touched on many fields and opened up entire new ones. And he wrote the most glorious prose: sinewy and graceful too.'

'And yet, he seems to have been a cold, unbending, devious man.'

'I don't know about devious. Subtle, certainly. And full of malice. He revelled in the unmasking of corruption and fraud; the unworthiness of the powerful was one of his cherished themes. And he loved to demolish his opponents, he was merciless. Perhaps no one with that talent for invective could resist using it. And yet there is such an encompassing compassion in his work—for the poor, the ignorant, the foolish, the brutalized.' She paused. '—Though it's rather an Olympian compassion.'

'Sounds like one of the intellectual icebergs. But strange fires can burn in those cold hearts.' He walked over to the writing-table. It was littered with piles of paper, whereas on the previous afternoon it had been bare. There were letters to Greenwood, copies of other people's correspondence, neat stacks of writing paper and envelopes, a thick manuscript boldly annotated in red, and, at one side by itself, a copy of the previous spring's history tripos with a note in Greenwood's vigorous handwriting clipped to the top. It said: 'Check R. Wing's *aegrotat*.' Below were written three names.

'What on earth is an *aegrotat?*' asked Edward.

Gillian peered over his shoulder. 'It's what you get if you can't take the examination but the authorities are satisfied that you would have passed it.'

'What? How does it work?'

'Well, suppose a student is too ill to sit the exam. Then if the appropriate committee is provided with satisfactory evidence that he would have passed, they grant him a pass, and he goes on exactly as if he had.'

'How stunningly simple. The bureaucratic mind hasn't taken over here, has it?'

'No, thank God. The system here is still personal—based on the assumption that people know each other, and the idea that anyone has met a high standard just by getting in. It's not an assembly line, so there isn't any need for a lot of rules to clog up everyone's life. A device like the *aegrotat* would be unthinkable at my university, but this is a different world. Personal trust is integral to the system, and trust saves a lot of time and trouble. Of course, the personal can be inequitable—'

'From where I sit, stuck in bureaucracy up to my neck like some character in a Beckett play, the rule book doesn't seem to be much of an answer. It's both inefficient and inequitable—the personal creeps through the interstices of the system every day.' He had picked up the exam and was flipping idly through its pages. 'I couldn't pass this.'

'I'm not sure I could, either. Unlike the Bourbons, I have learned much but have forgotten more.'

'What are these names, do you know them?'

Gillian glanced at the three names in Greenwood's note. 'Cooper-Hewson is an historian at King's. Q. Langdale I don't know; he's probably another person who taught Mr. Wing. They could vouch for the quality of his work, presumably. And T. Fox, that could be Toby—Bee's husband, you know. But I don't know why he'd be there, unless he's R. Wing's tutor.'

'Is Toby Fox an historian?'

'No. He's a physicist. But his field's irrelevant. As tutor, he wouldn't teach Wing; he'd be responsible for his general welfare, and he'd take care of things like the *aegrotat*.'

'Toby Fox was at that lunch on Sunday, wasn't he? I think I'll take this away with me,' said Edward thoughtfully. 'And I'd like to find out just how this *aegrotat* business works.'

'I don't know any more about it than I've told you. But Basil Peters could explain it. What are you thinking, anyway? What can this have to do with Greenwood's death?'

'I have no idea. It's just a connection, that's all.'

'Then you think that someone who was at lunch yesterday killed him this afternoon.'

'Don't you?'

'It's harder for me. I met all those people. They're not Xs to me.'

Before they turned to go, Gillian went to the table at the far end of the room and picked up one of the books reposing there. 'This is what Greenwood showed me yesterday.'

'Why is it special?'

'Look. It's a first edition of *The Decline and Fall*, beautifully bound, as you can see, and owned by Gibbon himself. Greenwood admired Gibbon greatly, and he saw himself, I think, as his intellectual heir, as upholding the Gibbonian tradition in a new dark age. You'd understand a lot about Greenwood if you read Gibbon.'

'Yes. I can just see myself telling the Superintendent that I'll solve our little mystery if he'll give me a fortnight off to read several thousand pages of Roman history. Let's go.'

CHAPTER 8

They drove back to Cambridge in silence. Gillian was exhausted, drained of words, thoughts, responses of any kind. Edward was absorbed in his own unquiet thoughts, turning over the strange debris left by a violent act. During the evening a chill had stolen into the air, and now a wind sprang up, blowing in fierce gusts that tore the leaves from the trees and sent them skittering wildly through the beams of his headlamps. Cambridge was dark, its narrow streets empty but for the occasional cyclist moving head down against the wind.

They went straight to the police station, where Gillian pulled herself together, gave her statement and signed it. Then Edward saw her to a taxi. He would probably be up most of the night, she knew. Her own wish, a strong one, was to go to bed immediately, but, unless Bee and Toby were both out, a discussion of the day's events was inevitable, and therefore Gillian had the taxi wait while she bought a bottle of whisky.

Grantchester Meadows was quiet in the silvery moonlight. After the taxi had departed, Gillian could hear someone playing a piano across the street. She fumbled for the key Bee had given her, and reluctantly, almost stealthily, opened the front door and stepped into the Stygian gloom of the hallway. Immediately, she was aware of muffled, angry talking coming from the end of the passage: from the kitchen, she thought, standing immobile in the dark, not wanting to listen, only caught by a profound wish to avoid the fray. There was an indistinguishable mutter, and then Bee's voice rising and falling in angry cadences.

Gillian remained frozen for a moment, as it passed through her mind that had Edward been there he would have continued to listen but that she could not so abuse Bee's hospitality. She turned back to the door and shut it noisily. In pitch-black silence she felt for the light switch. Then she clumped deliberately down the hall towards the kitchen, hearing over the sound of her own footsteps a renewed muttering. When she reached the kitchen, however, no one was there but Bee, who was banging the kettle about and carrying on an irascible monologue, her back to the doorway.

Gillian stopped at the door.

'*Joder*,' said Bee, whose studies in Hispanic literature had been broadened by summers on the coast of Spain where she had worked as a barmaid. 'I don't want bloody tea, I want brandy. A little oblivion, please, for Dr. Bee Hamilton, who prefers not to think about life any more today.' She turned and saw Gillian at the door. 'Oh. It's you. Where have you been?'

'With Edward,' Gillian replied vaguely, taking in Bee's strained look.

'Edward!' Bee was startled. 'You mean your Scotland Yard bloke? What's he doing here? Oh—did he come for your talk?'

'Yes. He did.'

Bee said in a hurried, embarrassed way, 'I'm sorry I didn't come. I meant to, but I couldn't start the bloody car, and by the time I'd given up trying, it was too late to walk. So I've been here, calling myself all kinds of a fool—for lots of reasons. Christ, I feel awful.'

'It's all right,' said Gillian. She didn't know what to make of Bee's performance; she felt certain that someone else had been there when she arrived. 'You can unplug the kettle; I've brought some whisky.'

'Have you? Thank God.' Bee went to a cupboard for some glasses, and Gillian glanced surreptitiously round the room. There were no obvious traces of a visitor, but the back door provided a handy exit into the night garden and the dank, dim pathways beyond. And there was the telephone, of course; it was in the kitchen. 'I wonder whether I should ring Basil,' Gillian said casually, walking over to the telephone and placing her hand briefly on the receiver. 'No. I suppose I don't need to until tomorrow.' The receiver was cool to her touch.

Bee poured two stiff whiskies. 'So. How did it go this afternoon?'

Gillian took her glass and stared abstractedly out through the kitchen windows. She could see nothing in the darkness. 'You haven't heard anything, I gather.'

'No. About what? What do you mean "heard anything"? Did some old chauvinist die of apoplexy?'

'Not exactly. Alistair Greenwood was shot. And he's dead.'

'Greenwood? Shot? Jesus Christ! What happened?'

'Somebody shot him at King's—at my talk, during the applause at the end. Nobody saw who it was.'

'Christ!' Bee said again. She gulped down her drink. 'I can't believe it. He's actually dead?'

'Yes. He was dead before the ambulance got there.' Gillian downed some whisky while Bee poured herself another large one.

'Did you see it happen?'

'More or less. I was standing only a few feet from him, but I wasn't looking at him when he fell over. Everyone in the audience saw it, though.'

'Tell me.'

Gillian told Bee the story in bare outline, omitting for reasons not entirely clear to herself her visit with Edward to Greenwood's house. Through her exhaustion, she attempted to gauge Bee's reactions, sensing beneath the appearance of shock and excitement something more intense and personal.

'I can't believe he's gone,' Bee said twice, and it seemed to Gillian an odd choice of word, as if Greenwood had been a sort of obstacle in a path Bee had mapped out for herself.

'Who was there?' she asked, and Gillian told her the names she knew, none of which induced a visible reaction. It was the freakish chance of Edward's presence in the audience that fascinated Bee. 'What a nasty shock for the murderer. Have you told Edward about our little lunch party yesterday?' she asked, pouring herself a third drink.

'Of course.'

Bee laughed, her words coming a little unevenly. 'So will the mysterious Fiona be arrested, or will the whole jolly crew be suspects A to E?'

'I've no idea,' Gillian said flatly, thinking that the whisky had not dulled Bee's wits. Bee leaned back, tipping her chair against the wall. 'You know, when you came in, I was imagining putting Greenwood in front of a firing squad. Well. What a show. The king is dead. And so much for your lyrical memories of the cloister.' She didn't bother to conceal her satisfaction and at that moment Gillian thoroughly disliked her and thought she would write off the friendship. What had been there fifteen years ago was sunk too many fathoms deep for a salvage operation; diving into the wreck, she found nothing but corrosion and silt. She decided to go upstairs.

Then the front door banged, and Toby hurtled into the kitchen, breathless and excited. 'Gillian! Thank goodness you're here, you can tell me what's going on. I've just heard some garbled tale that Alistair Greenwood was shot this afternoon. At a meeting of the Historical Society. That can't be true.'

'It's perfectly true.'

'I can't believe it. Where did it happen? Jesus!' he added violently.

'Not Jesus, King's,' said Bee, leering.

'Shut up, Bee. Pour me a drink, for God's sake.' Surprisingly, she did so and gave it to him without comment.

Then they both sat at the kitchen table with the bottle and their glasses and a cardboard box of Toby's papers which nobody thought of moving. Gillian sat down too, knowing that she couldn't go to bed until Toby had heard the story. She furnished him with the same abbreviated version Bee had received, and concluded, 'So at the moment, nobody knows who shot him, or why.'

'And why the Chetwynd Room, for the love of God?' said Toby. 'It's appalling. And it must have been horribly risky. Why not at his house?'

'God knows.' Gillian finished her whisky and did not pour another. Any more, she told herself, and she would be sure to wake up at three in the morning. And tonight she did not want to face three-in-the-morning thoughts.

'Fiona must have done it,' Toby asserted. He leaned back and lit a cigarette. 'The question is, why?'

'Maybe it was a political gesture,' said Bee.

'Political? Don't be a bloody idiot. This is Cambridge, not Berkeley. What are you on about?'

'A symbolic act. An act of public significance.'

'As opposed to a private hatred?' asked Gillian.

'Yes. I don't have to tell you that Greenwood stood for a lot of things that a lot of people wanted destroyed. That need destroying. And,' Bee added with slurred emphasis, 'I'm glad he's dead, and I don't propose to make a pious pretence of feeling sorry.'

'Don't, then. But have the decency to keep quiet about it,' Toby snapped.

'Don't talk to me about decency.'

They were off again, Gillian thought wearily. 'Fiona Clay's the type to go to bed with revolutionaries, not be one,' Toby went on. 'But she pointed a gun at Greenwood yesterday, and today he's dead. One can't ignore a sequence like that.'

'Why do you think she killed him then? Because he was rude to her at lunch?' asked Gillian.

'Unless she's a lunatic, there's more to it than that.'

'What?'

'I can think of only one thing.'

Bee began to laugh. 'Perhaps the peacock's tail isn't just feathers after all.' Suddenly, she and Toby seemed to be on good terms.

Gillian could stand no more. She went upstairs to her room, undressed carelessly and fell into bed. Nothing made sense. Toby and Bee: what was she to make of them? Was either of them capable of murder? She didn't know; they had become different people since she had known them well. Edward might observe, if she could recount to him all the conversations of the past two days, that the murderer—if it were one of them—had been wise to avoid feigning a sorrow he did not feel.

The exhaustion that follows shock claimed her. She sank into a half-dream in which Edward and Greenwood and crowds of men in black gowns flapping like ravens' wings were all confused. Then she was aware of nothing at all.

CHAPTER 9

Shortly before sunrise the next morning, a student who had been up all night writing an essay jogged sleepily up the path across Coe Fen and along the river towards the footbridge that crossed it at Mill Lane. Just before the bridge, the water spilled shallowly over a weir. Large, ugly chunks of cement segmented the weir, and the waters of the Cam curled past them, dropping several feet before rushing through the narrow passage beneath the bridge and then resuming their calm flow beyond it. From there, the river travelled gently on past the college Backs, beneath bridges and willow trees, and eventually past Cambridge to the north, where it joined the Ouse and meandered through the fens, emptying finally into the desolate Wash.

It had been a pretty river once, full of secretive variety: shallows and deep pools, shadowy recesses beneath the roots of old trees, and green, wavering weedy places. Then the engineers came, and they saw—not a river but a drainage system: a means, they said, of improving agricultural production by controlling the water table. To this end, they did their best to make the river resemble a drainpipe. They dredged it and scraped it to achieve a uniform depth, they smoothed its banks, expunging irregularities, and they built weirs and lowered the level of the water. The small, interconnected subaqueous worlds disappeared, taking life with them. The river turned mud brown and sullen, and from then on flowed opaque and silent between its even banks.

The student trotted wearily up the path along the water's edge, breathing heavily. On the other bank, the boatyard was almost empty in late October, but a few punts were still herded together, moving very slightly. He slowed and gave them a nostalgic glance, thinking of warm summer afternoons as he thudded by in the chill dawn. Then, with a remnant of will and wind, he ran the rest of the way to the bridge. There he stopped and leaned on the low wall, drawing heavy breaths and sweating. As he breathed, he gazed down at the water purling over the weir, thinking of nothing in particular. Then his eye was caught by an odd shape just under the water's curve. He stared at it in half-puzzled disbelief. It was long and pale, its wavering shape distorted by the movement of the water. He couldn't see well in the grey light. Leaning over the wall, he stared harder at the shape, amazement turning to fright as he watched the peculiar, fluttering object resolve itself into a hand. He saw a thumb and fingers; the fingers moved against the weir, exploring it tenderly, attentively, as a blind woman might feel her lover's face. He saw nothing more; the wrist receded into the grim, brown water.

The student gave a hoarse cry, and ran. He ran up to the end of Mill Lane and seeing no one there ran across the middle of the town to Regent Street, hoping to see a constable. But Regent Street was empty, so he ran the rest of the way to the police station. As he burst in, gasping like a messenger from Marathon, the sky turned from pearl to blue, and the day began.

Gillian got up late that morning, groggy and stale after an uneasy sleep. She drew the curtains and looked out at the empty street. Rain had come and gone during the night; surfaces gleamed wetly, and sodden copper beech leaves, as dark as old bloodstains, were pasted against the curb. A chill fog lay over the fields near the river, but above, the sky was clear and cool, and the sun was shining brilliantly again, as if proving itself a reliable fixture of the Cambridge autumn.

Alone in the kitchen, Gillian made some coffee and drank it scalding hot, trying to clear her brain. As she poured a second cup, the telephone rang, and, after a moment's hesitation, she answered it. Edward's voice came crisply over the wires. Gillian knew that tone; detached and neutral, it was like a surgeon's glove: it separated him from his subject without hampering delicate operations. His policeman's voice—she wondered what was up.

'Can you come round this morning?' he asked. 'We've been hard at it for the last twelve hours. There are some things I'd like to tell you.'

'I'll be there,' she responded, matching his tone. 'What time?'

'As soon as you can. Half an hour?'

'All right.' She waited for the line to go dead then, but he said, suddenly sounding more human, 'I haven't had any sleep.'

'I know.'

'In half an hour, then.' The telephone clicked.

A few minutes later, Gillian set off. The police station, formerly in Regent Street in a soot-encrusted turn-of-the-century building, had moved to larger, modern headquarters at the far corner of Parker's Piece. The quickest way lay along Fen Causeway, reeking and noisy with traffic, and Gillian chose a more circuitous route.

Everything looked the same as it had the day before, as if nothing had happened. The little houses were silent, but Grantchester Street was busy with morning shoppers trundling in and out of the post office and the tiny shops, buying lamb chops and vegetables, soap and cigarettes and milk. The door to the butcher's shop was open, and Gillian heard laughter as she passed.

She grew warm as she walked; the sun had power in it although November was close at hand. The stretches of green in Lammas Land were empty and quiet, the cows in the fen seemed not to have moved, and the dun waters of the Cam slid lazily towards the sea, calm and opaque, as if all memory and grief could be borne away on the bosom of the current.

The footbridge was busy, as usual, with students and shoppers and a few late tourists. A policeman was there too, standing immobile with his back to the weir. Gillian, whose mind was far away, gave him little thought and hurried on up Mill Lane and into Pembroke Street. She passed the dark walls of Pembroke College, a little parade of the last half-dozen centuries, and then the stone archway that guarded a tiny, coveted space where the fellows parked their cars. She glanced casually in as she went by, and then she stopped, her eye caught by the stonework. It was a pretty gateway, but what Gillian had noticed was the condition of the stone. The surface was black and leprous and here and there had buckled and peeled like the skin of a charred fish. Where the dead skin had curled away or fallen, rough patches of the stone's natural golden hue were bared, like a fish's delicate flesh. But these, too, were horribly diseased, the stone soft and friable. Gillian tentatively touched a patch and watched dismayed as a little trickle of sandy particles cascaded from beneath her fingers. Thinking of Toby's remarks on the upkeep of old college buildings, she walked swiftly on past the ugly great rump of Lion Yard, through the centre of the city to Parker's Piece, a wide, flat common fringed by pretty nineteenth-century terraces. She crossed the damp turf to the police station on the far side. As she had vaguely noticed the previous evening, it was a dull, graceless building faced with brick below and a composite of sharp stones, grey as a janitor's mop, above. Inside, however, it was unexpectedly pleasant. The main foyer, where she waited for Edward after giving her name, was light and airy and unintimidating. It was also busy. Uniformed men and women eddied through; a student was describing a stolen bicycle, while next to him a pathetic, rumpled little man wearing plastic sandals over extremely dirty socks mumbled indistinctly and listened to a middle-aged officer's patient replies. Another man, with a close-

shaven head and a battered briefcase, tossed some papers on
the counter and left, pausing at the door to offer a wry jibe
about job satisfaction. Gillian inspected the white walls and
the glass front that faced the common, the rubber-tiled floor
and the identification chart for lost dogs. The police station
was not beautiful, but it was reassuring.

Then one of the doors behind her opened, and Edward
came out. He escorted her upstairs to the room he was using.
It was small, but the window looked over the common, wide
and peaceful in the sunlight. The inevitable metal filing
cabinets were there, but their grim, institutional presence
was defeated by the shining wooden floor and the wooden
desk by the window. Edward looked tired and tense; the lines
around his eyes were deeper than usual, and there was a hint
of grey pallor in his skin. He had been drinking too much
nasty coffee; a litter of disposable cups and unused packets
of sugar lay about.

'You're the same colour as your filing cabinets,' Gillian
remarked affably on entering.

Edward glanced at them. 'I feel about that colour, too,'
he said. 'Sit down.'

Gillian sat. 'Well?' she asked. Edward went to the window
and stood looking out, unsmiling, his hands in his pockets,
his body half-turned away from her.

'There's been another death,' he said in his policeman's
voice. 'A body was found in the river this morning.'

'In the river?' Gillian repeated stupidly. She was thinking
with sudden panic that she hadn't seen Bee since the previous
evening.

'Yes. By the footbridge at Mill Lane. It was jammed against
the weir.'

'Oh God. The policeman there—'

'Yes,' Edward said curtly.

Edward had had a bad morning. He had been up all night,
which was not unusual in his line of work but which did not
improve his outlook on life, and then another body had

turned up. Another body in another very public place. He had gone down to the river in the cold dawn to see it hauled up, a pale, dripping, clumsy load. Then he had helped to search the banks nearby. Nothing had been found, of course, and men had been sent to look further upstream. Afterwards, he had needed to clean himself up. He had fished his shaving tackle out of his car, where, forlornly wrapped in its tissue paper beneath an old blanket, still lay, unbroached, the bottle of Bollinger he had brought to drink with Gillian. He had thought to celebrate her lecture and to sever himself from his work for a little while, and neither had proved possible. Love and policework were out of joint, and not for the first time. He had gone back to the station, shaved and drunk more coffee. And now Gillian was here, and they would have to sit in a bare little room talking of murder.

'Who is it?' Gillian was asking.

'A young woman with black and magenta hair. She corresponds quite precisely to your description of Fiona Clay.'

'And she's dead? Drowned, I mean?'

'So far as we know. The PM will tell us.'

'Oh God, Edward. How horrible.' Gillian stared at him, the colour washing out of her face.

'Yes. It's bloody awful,' he said, renewed anger at the violence and waste breaking through his fatigue and his years of experience. It was as if Gillian's countenance, pale with the shocks of the last eighteen hours, were a personal reproach, although he knew that this was unreasonable. He was a good detective. Presented with the problem of a death, he was clever, efficient, at times brilliant at producing the solution. But even as he was gripped by the fascinating logic of pursuit, he was captive audience to the aftermath of the initial, murderous act. No act was an island; murderer and victim were connected to the larger social organism in myriad ways, and violence seeped like poison through the interstitial membranes. At moments—this was one—being a good cop was not enough.

Gillian was speaking. 'Why did she drown? What happened?'

'We don't know yet. We haven't even confirmed her identity. But there isn't much doubt. And I may as well tell you now, it looks as if she shot Professor Greenwood. We've found the gun.'

'Where?'

'In her shoulder-bag. She was wearing it slung across her body, so it didn't come off.'

'But why would she kill him?' Gillian protested.

Edward shrugged. 'I don't know yet.' The telephone rang. He picked it up and listened impassively, thanked the caller and replaced the receiver.

'Denham Greenwood has just identified Fiona Clay. He came up from London last night after he was told of his brother's death. I had only a few words with him. He's on his way here now.'

'Poor man,' said Gillian. 'Two shocks like that in a row. Did he know her very well?'

'Apparently not. We had to ask him last night, because we were trying to find her. He gave us the address of her flat in Hampstead. She wasn't there, of course, but the flat's been searched now, and they found quite a pharmacopoeia there. Miss Clay liked drugs, seemingly.'

'What kind?'

'Oh, several kinds. There was a whacking great jar of cocaine, I'm told, and a lot of pills. Thorazine, I believe, and various uppers and downers, and some caps of amyl nitrite.'

'Was she a dealer, do you think?'

'Quite possibly. That might explain the gun. But at the moment, I'm more interested in the extent to which she may have scrambled her own brains.'

Gillian nodded. 'Yes, I see what...But where does Alistair Greenwood come in? He doesn't fit.'

Edward came away from the window and sat on the desk near Gillian, arms folded. 'What do you know of Greenwood's private life?'

'Nothing.'

'Precisely.'

Gillian gave an incredulous snort. 'If you think he was mixed up with some underworld of drugs and guns—'

'I don't,' said Edward. 'It's not necessary to think of anything so outré. But he kept his personal life completely hidden. He may have been fanatically private, of course, but in the circumstances, it's not illogical to assume that he was concealing something he considered discreditable. Fiona Clay wouldn't have done much for his image as the austere philosopher king, would she? Even if he knew nothing about her less savoury activities. There's got to be a connection there, and we'll keep looking until we find it.' He glanced down at his watch. 'Denham Greenwood will be here at any moment. I may see you for dinner this evening, if nothing urgent comes up just then. I'll let you know later. But I did want to tell you about Fiona Clay myself.'

'Thank you.' As Gillian got up to go, there was a tap on the door. A constable stuck his head in, and Edward had a hurried word with him. Then he motioned Gillian towards the corridor.

'They've found a black, spike-heeled shoe stuck in the river bank. It could be hers; the other one hasn't been found. It's probably at the bottom of the river.'

'So she might have just been in a daze and stumbled in?'

'Perhaps. Suicide seems unlikely, unless she drugged herself first. The river's too shallow, and anyhow a suicide wouldn't have left one shoe.'

Gillian frowned. 'You know, Edward, that's not how she wore her shoulder-bag at lunch. She was wearing it dangling from one shoulder.'

'She was probably afraid of losing it last night.'

'I suppose so.'

They reached the end of the corridor, and Edward said in a resigned way, 'We'll be releasing some information to the press today, so be prepared for the gamut of scandalous speculation about Professor Greenwood and the unusual Miss Clay.'

'Oh God. Must you?'

'It can't be helped, you know that.'

'I'm sorry. I can't bear to think of it. Leering, prurient, vulgar articles, how the mighty are fallen, etc., etc. Toby and Bee were smacking their lips over it last night.'

'Were they? Who mentioned it first?'

'Toby. But they were just speculating along the same lines as you—'

'Did anything about the conversation suggest that they knew she was dead?'

'No.'

'And how did they react to Alistair Greenwood's murder?'

Gillian told him, but her discomfort at being so awkwardly placed made her add defensively, 'You can't seriously think that either of them killed Greenwood.'

'I'm obliged to consider the possibilities that are presented to me, however unpleasant they may be. It's part of the job.'

Gillian was instantly remorseful. 'I'm sorry. Forget I said that. It's just that I don't want to consider unpleasant possibilities.'

'It should be over soon,' was Edward's only reply, but their constraint lifted indistinctly, like the hem of a cloud.

Chapter 10

Edward went back to his office. He gathered up the dirty cups and put the various files he had been reading into a tidy pile. As he did this, he organized two files in his mind, one containing things he knew, the other things he knew he wanted to know. He hoped that Denham Greenwood was going to tell him some of the things he wanted to know, particularly about Fiona Clay.

A few minutes later, he met Denham in the main foyer and escorted him to one of the interview rooms, which were small, rather barren rooms in the security unit, located near the cells. A uniformed sergeant followed them in and retired to a corner to take inconspicuous notes. Denham inspected this grim environment with indifference and sat down, arms folded. He was composed, but his clothes were creased and tension was visible in the slight bulge of his jaw muscles. Edward studied him. A big man, he had a smooth, rather highly coloured complexion, light blue eyes, pale hair that had receded from an already high forehead, and an alert, dominating presence. He liked expensive objects; Edward had seen the tomato-red Lagonda outside, looking marvellously conspicuous and implausible among the other cars, like a huge tropical bird in a flock of sparrows. There was more to it than possessions, though. Denham smelled of money: a deliberate, undiluted musk, like the base ingredient of a perfume without its rare and delicate overlays.

The interview went smoothly enough. Edward began by asking about Fiona Clay.

'I can't tell you very much about her, I'm afraid,' Denham said. 'I met her only a couple of weeks ago. At a party in Chelsea. I liked the way she looked.' (Another expensive, racy object, Edward thought.) 'I took her out several times; she had a flat in Hampstead, a nice enough little place, and she said she was a model. I assumed she was—she certainly looked like one. Her clothes were right: a bit wild, but expensive. And she said she was an actress, too. That probably meant she'd been an extra in some films. I had no idea she carried a gun around.'

'Did you know she had drugs in her flat?'

'No. What kind of drugs?'

'Cocaine. Some other things.'

'No. I didn't know. But it wouldn't surprise me. It's nothing unusual. And she did seem pretty unstable sometimes.'

'What do you mean?'

'Oh, she was the histrionic type—unpredictable fits of temper, sulks—she was always way up or way down.'

'What induced you to bring her to Cambridge?' Edward asked with real curiosity.

'She did. I mentioned that I was going up for lunch on Sunday, and she asked me to take her. And, God help me, I thought that it would be rather a good joke. I thought she'd give those staid academics a jolt. A jolt! Christ! She frightened the wits out of them—and me. I don't know what would have happened if Pamela hadn't grabbed her arm. And now my brother is dead and she's drowned herself in the river or something. Do you think she shot him?'

'It looks that way, but nothing is certain yet.'

Denham passed his hand tiredly over his face. 'I don't understand it at all.'

'Could she have known your brother before you met her?' Edward asked. 'Did you have any indication at all of a past connection between them? Could she have gone to that party in Chelsea in order to meet you?'

Denham looked faintly startled. 'I don't know. That hadn't occurred to me.'

'What about her behaviour at your brother's house? Was there anything to suggest—apart from the incident with the gun—that she knew him?'

'I don't know. I didn't suspect anything, so I wasn't paying attention, except when we arrived. You should have seen their faces. Alistair hardly looked at her. He was cold, and rude in that frightfully polished way that no one combats with any success. I thought she'd think he was quaint and not give a damn what he or anybody else said. Instead, she panicked— or something—and got drunk. That was ghastly enough. Then she pulled a gun on him. It was unbelievable.'

'Go on.'

'I thought she was just trying to scare them—to pay them back for being snobs. I never guessed there was something between her and Alistair. She wanted to go to Cambridge just for a giggle, I thought. It's quite pleasant in the Lagonda.'

'I'm sure it is,' Edward said, his voice dry. His own MG was developing a new and ominous rattle.

'But after we left, when we got into the car, we had a row. You can imagine. I nearly gave her the hobnailed boot and told her to walk back to London. I asked her what the hell she'd been playing at, and she said it was none of my business. And I grabbed her and said what the hell do you mean, you could have killed somebody. She sort of flounced and muttered something about snotty old farts and nobody had a right to treat her like that. Then she passed out again. Christ almighty, what the hell was I supposed to do? I drove back to London.'

'Did you think she was hiding something?'

'I didn't know what to think. I just thought she was crazy. But now—'

'What sort of link could she have had with your brother?'

'I really couldn't say.'

'You weren't aware of any predilection of your brother's for, er—'

Denham cut him off. 'No, never. It was not the sort of thing he would ever have allowed me to know.'

'Why did he keep the gun?'

A sour little smile flickered across Denham's countenance. 'Alistair was always like that. He kept his own counsel, and he had no regard for the plebeian authorities.'

'Did you think of calling the police yourself?'

'Good God no. I know my brother, and frankly, I wouldn't have cared to interfere.'

Edward went over the ground again, carefully, and he extracted various details about the Chelsea party, Fiona's range of acquaintances, and her behaviour at the Sunday lunch, but Denham had nothing of real substance to add. So Edward passed on to the matter of Denham's movements on Sunday and Monday. Denham was cool and business-like; it was quickly apparent that he was a busy man who liked to keep many financial plates in the air at once. On Sunday, he had driven up to Cambridge for lunch, something he did two or three times a year. After the scene in the dining-room, he had taken Fiona to the car, had the row with her, and then driven straight back to London. He'd left her in front of her flat and hadn't seen her since. He'd gone home, had a shower, made some telephone calls, and later met a friend for a few drinks. Then he'd spent the night with a woman. On Monday morning he'd been in the City, attending several meetings and answering a dozen urgent telephone calls. After lunch—another meeting—he had returned home and worked there. He frequently did so when he needed to concentrate; there were fewer interruptions at home. He had a secretary who came to his house when he needed her. He'd shut himself up with some contracts at three or four o'clock and had worked straight through until about 7:30. He'd been having a quiet drink at 8:00 when the constable had knocked at the door and told him about his brother. Sometime after that, he'd put some things in a suitcase and driven back to Cambridge. He supposed he'd got there between 10:30 and midnight; he didn't know.

Edward did know; he'd arrived at the police station at 11.20. So he had probably started driving shortly after 10:00. That made sense, as he would have needed some time to recover from the shock. Once in Cambridge, he had seen his brother's body and had then checked in to a hotel for the remainder of the night. Edward told Denham that his statement would have to be verified, and Denham furnished him with the names of the relevant secretaries.

'There's one other matter I'd like to ask you about,' Edward said. 'Your brother's will. Do you know how he left his property?'

Denham gave him a measuring look. 'No, I don't,' he said coolly. 'The living members of the family are myself, my sister Mary and her husband, and Pamela Ditton. There's a substantial estate involved, of course. Large enough to tempt a legatee. He could have divided it between my sister and myself, or left it all to the college cat.'

Soon after that, Denham left. He would be available in London, he said, should the police want anything further. Edward went back upstairs to his little room and looked out of the window at the green common, now criss-crossed with cyclists and pedestrians. He considered Denham Greenwood: a tough, able, aggressive man, a power in his own world, though hardly a blazing star like his brother. He took a certain pleasure in an intelligent risk; he was astute and cynical. Edward made a note to ask the Yard to run a quick check on Denham's finances. He didn't know what was in the will—or so he said—but he might have made assumptions. There was probably nothing in it, but it would be interesting if Denham turned out to be dangerously over-extended, as princes of finance often were.

Edward was curious about the will, and he felt a tug of irritation. Waiting for vital pieces of information was not something to which he ever became reconciled. He would have it that evening, he told himself, and, meanwhile, he would not be short of things to do. First, he would go back to the river and examine the place where the shoe was found. Pamela Ditton was to see him early in the afternoon, and after that he wanted to look around Alistair Greenwood's rooms in college. He left the room, shutting the door behind him, and went in search of Superintendent Hardy.

Gillian, meanwhile, walked aimlessly about, not knowing what to do with her distress. By noon she felt calmer and, passing an inviting pub, thought she would stop for a drink and even something to eat. The Free Press was dark, cosy and already crowded inside. There were several small rooms, all filled with noisy, cheerful people. Behind the bar, a man and a woman moved with dexterous speed, chatting to the customers, most of whom they seemed to know. Gillian looked in vain for a place to sit down, and then she heard her name. Pamela Ditton was sitting at a table in the corner. She had some cider and a meat pie in front of her, and she was alone. Gillian ordered a ploughman's lunch and brought a glass of wine to the table, while Pamela squeezed along the wooden seat to make room for her.

'Hullo, Gillian,' she said sombrely. 'If you're wondering what I'm doing here, I'm fortifying myself. I have to go to the police station this afternoon and answer questions about Alistair.'

'I'm sorry. It must be the last thing you feel like doing.'

'Yes, it is, rather. But I don't suppose it will take long. I haven't anything to tell them.' She sipped her cider and set the mug down in a new position, leaving a wet ring where it had previously stood. This she slowly traced round and round with her finger as they talked.

'Poor Cousin Alistair. How well did you know him?'

'Not well at all. I admired him from afar. I'd never had a conversation with him until Sunday.'

'I've known him since I was a child. I was terrified of him then. He was so scornful. But we saw each other rather often after I came here—he did have a sense of family, in his way. And we have—had, I mean—a sort of irritable fondness for one another. I feel bereft.'

'I'm sorry,' Gillian replied. What else could she say? Her disquieting conversation with Edward lingered, and she thought of unpleasant possibilities. Yet if Pamela were grieving it would be monstrous to doubt her. 'His books will immortalize him, and that's probably what he wanted most,' she offered.

Pamela nodded and drank more cider, leaving her meat pie untouched. 'Denham won't be breaking his heart, anyhow. Alistair always made him feel a fool.'

'Well, he was one on Sunday.'

'You mean Fiona. Yes, he should have known better. Whatever he did, he could never impress Alistair, or put him out of countenance, either. I'm sure Alistair got the upper hand when he was still in the cradle. Denham's not in the same class.'

'He's done well in his own way.'

'Oh yes—he's a financial wizard and loves talking about his clever deals. You saw the Lagonda—he's got a big Mercedes too, and a house in St John's Wood, and a flat in Majorca, and I don't know what else. He's always having dinner at Annabel's. But then he comes up here, and Alistair looks down his nose. Cambridge makes it worse, of course.'

'Worse?'

'Oh, well, it's Alistair's kingdom, and Denham wasn't even an undergraduate here.'

'Why not?'

'Would you have come up, if Alistair were only two years behind you and had made your life intolerable at school?'

'I see. But there's Oxford.'

'Denham wasn't really Oxbridge material. And what if Alistair had chosen Oxford after all?'

Gillian digested that while Pamela bit into her meat pie, grimaced and pushed away her plate. 'I can't eat,' she said. The ploughman's lunch arrived, and Gillian nibbled at it, feeling embarrassed, as though she ought to be unable to eat, too.

'Do the police know all about Sunday?' Pamela asked suddenly.

'I gave them a fairly complete account, I think.'

'The Scotland Yard bloke is a friend of yours, isn't he?'

Gillian, weary of circumspection, suppressed a wish to say baldly: 'No. He's my lover,' and merely nodded. Pamela would find out soon enough, if she hadn't already.

'What do the police think? They must think Fiona killed him.'

'I don't know,' Gillian replied in a discouraging tone.

'She's the logical suspect, of course. But I'd rather it was Victor Smallbone. Ugh—what a toad.'

'A toad, certainly. But a homicidal toad?'

'He was a student of Alistair's,' said Pamela darkly. 'Any of them could be homicidal—though they're more likely to be suicidal. Anyhow, I just hope the police settle the business quickly. It would be so ghastly to have them sniffing about for weeks, asking questions, making Cambridge a perfect bear garden.'

Gillian felt a stab of resentment on Edward's behalf but saw no point in replying. Pamela drained her cider. 'I must leave, I'm afraid. I've got to go along to the police station.'

Gillian finished her lunch alone, wishing she weren't in the middle of the investigation. She liked Pamela; she didn't enjoy wondering whether she had murdered her cousin, nor the nervous hostility that erupted when people thought she had inside information that she wouldn't pass on. Ten to one, she thought, Pamela knows about Edward and me. And that probably means she's talked to Bee. I wonder when.

She walked back through the centre of the town and up to Clare, on her way to the University Library. The library was across the river, and she wanted to avoid King's and the footbridge at Mill Lane. On Clare bridge she paused and leaned on the parapet, watching the dappled water below and wondering what it would be like to be part of Cambridge again.

Only three months earlier, at the height of the summer, she had flown to London, leaving the University of the Pacific

Northwest's history department to get on without her for a
year. She was ready for her leave: as head of the department,
she had been attending far too many meetings, and she felt
stale. It had been a long journey. Vancouver, Lotus-land of
Canada, seemed far away from everywhere and was infinitely
distant now. In this ancient little town, the entire North
American continent grew remote. Supposing she were offered
a job here, was Cambridge what she wanted? Was this where
she would do her best work and find a sense of place? She
found herself thinking of home, of the drive up the Hudson
and her mother. She had stopped in New York on her way to
London and had rented a car. Her mother rarely ventured
into the city and in any case would not have considered it a
proper visit had Gillian not come home.

Her mother was old now, but lived on alone in the tall,
white wooden house Gillian had grown up in. Nothing had
changed there; Gillian still loved to return to it. Her visit
had been characteristic. She had arrived; her mother had been
glad to see her. She stayed for three days. Through the
windows she saw the same green swell of meadow, flecked
with buttercups and daisies and Queen Anne's lace, black-
eyed susans and butter-and-eggs. Someone's sheep grazed in
the field beyond the unused barn; she could see them biting
the lush grass near the brook. As a girl, she had sometimes
seen deer in the fields in the early morning, and often in the
winter she had looked out of her window when she awoke to
see their delicate hoofprints in the snow.

It was cool inside the house, even in June, as though better
to preserve its contents. Her mother, warmly dressed, sat on
the shabby sofa, enveloped by the familiar: the thin Persian
rugs on the wide-planked floor, the grand piano, the shelves
of worn books, the pictures, the luminous marble bust of
mother and child, their two heads embraced within one pure
white curve. The sitting-room was large and well propor-
tioned, with a high ceiling; it felt spacious despite the clutter.
The wide sills beneath the windows, the tables, the bookcases

and the piano were buried in a litter of framed photographs and letters and family treasures that had accumulated over the long years like the gentle rain of microscopic bodies that sifts downward through the seas and covers their beds with a rich and nourishing debris. There were the shells Gillian had collected on Cape Cod, jars filled with beach glass, silver candlesticks, drawings, tiny ivory elephants, a painted brass peacock, bowls of flowers, and an arrangement of stuffed birds in brilliant plumage, elaborately immobile in their Victorian glass case, which rested, improbably, on top of the television.

At seventy, Gillian's mother was frail but not sad. She spoke gently and repetitively of the past. She was still amused by it; she remembered life as an adventure. Gillian, listening to her, handing her a stiff scotch, thought how calm she seemed. She herself had felt calm at moments, as though she were at last in control or as though fate had briefly lost interest in her, but it had been illusory; she had always found herself storm-tossed again, thrashing about in a surprisingly rough sea. Should she say something about Edward, she wondered.

The moment did not immediately present itself; her mother was reminiscing comfortably and preferred talking to listening. Just then she was somewhere in the Thirties, crossing the Atlantic. Gillian half listened to the tales of what she thought of as her mother's Fitzgerald period; she had heard them before and was more interested in looking for signs of fatigue or strain or loneliness. There was no point in asking; her mother always said she was fine. Some month, some year, nevertheless, she might find it too much to go on living alone, and Gillian did not want to be caught unprepared.

She regarded her parent with uncritical affection; the time for criticism was long past. Her mother sat upright, thin legs drawn up beneath her, hands gesturing. Her hair was parted in the centre and drawn back into a bun. It was quite grey, and her skin was a dense pattern of fine wrinkles, but her hands and her voice and her large, deep brown eyes were still quick with life. She seemed to have changed very little in the past few years. Gillian was reassured. England was really no further away than Vancouver, but it might have seemed so.

Gillian had been living in Vancouver for nearly a dozen years, to her own continued surprise. 'Don't go,' friends in Toronto had said; 'your brain will get mouldy.' In New York they had said 'Where?' and when told, used what they knew— California—merely blanketing the image with eternal snows. This was hardly accurate, eternal rains would have come closer to the mark, but Gillian had soon abandoned any attempt to explain. New Yorkers would continue to ask 'Where?' and their curiosity would continue to be entirely satiated by the simple reply 'North of California.' To add 'on the west coast of Canada' was to supply too much information. Being an Easterner herself, Gillian accepted this as a justifiable absence of interest in the provinces, whereas the parochial complacency of Vancouver's citizenry she regarded with annoyed incredulity.

Yet she stayed, for she had a good job when academic jobs were scarce. She painstakingly constructed a life. Her work prospered, she found a house, she found friends. She and the city grew towards each other, travelling a little distance each year, like converging glaciers. But she remained an Easterner, drawn back to the little stony fields of New England and the electric density of big eastern cities, so different from the slack, suburban air of Vancouver.

Possibly it was the continued sense of floating, adjusted but unattached, unrooted in the place where she lived and worked, that kept warm her interest in the migrations of empire, in the colonial settlers, who had chosen to build new lives in alien terrain. She had never felt like a colonial herself, although she had been called one in Cambridge. She had been taken aback, then amused, by the epithet; it had started her thinking about the imperial idea and its sclerotic anomalies. She was not sure what she did feel like. She thought of herself as both American and Canadian, or as neither. She was, by blood, half Canadian, and that seemed to mean something, or why would she feel an irrational satisfaction in plying her talents in Canada rather than in the more obvious place? Her father, scion of a staid and respectable United Empire Loyalist family in Toronto, had chosen, in a moment of independence—or aberration, according to the family—to work in New York. Within a year he had met her mother; and together they bought the large piece of land up the Hudson and the handsome white Federalist house. Gillian lived there until she was fourteen. Then her parents moved back to Toronto. But they kept the house, staying there in the summers, and when Gillian's father died, her mother chose to leave the warm bosom of her relations and return to what she called the farm. It was a place that was her own, she said. And she had never liked the family houses in Rosedale, massive brick edifices, 'too heavy and solid and worthy,' she said, 'like banks.' Her husband's family, who were bankers, shrugged, inured by the years to her eccentricities. Gillian was pleased and not at all alarmed by the decision. The farm was home, and her mother had friends there.

Oddly enough, it was the winters of her childhood that Gillian remembered best, though the summers had been rich. She liked the bare, wooded hills in winter, stony underfoot and rustling with dead leaves, the trees still, dun-brown skeletons accepting the snow that fell between them. Sometimes frost would follow thaw in the night and coat all the trees with ice. Then, as the sun rose over the fields the crowns of the hills would blaze with freezing fire, flashing and glittering, each separate notched twig cast in gold, like the forest in one of the fairytales Gillian spent her winter evenings reading.

The famous New England fall, crackling blue skies and brilliant leaves, she did not remember with love. The woods were filled with hunters then, blundering about, murdering

things, making her own territory into enemy ground. Signs—
NO HUNTING NO TRESPASSING—were posted on trees
and fences, but the hunters disregarded them. Neighbours
lost cows and sheep every year; in the hunters' fierce,
bourbon-soaked vision, anything from a horse to an
automobile was worth putting a bullet into, on the off-
chance. Loud voices and the crack of rifles echoed in the
woods. Gillian, huddled in her window seat, searched the
trees for glimpses of red jackets and thought of pits and snares.
There had been a story in the newspaper one year, when
Gillian was ten. Two brothers had come up from the city to
hunt and had shot each other. She had read it with angry,
bloodthirsty pleasure and had carried it about for weeks.

Sitting with her mother, gazing out at the summery
meadow, Gillian thought how much she missed this country
when she was in the west, with its rain and its everlasting
bloody evergreens. She wondered whether she would come
home again one day, when she was old. But, unlike her
mother, she did not have friends here; her friends were
scattered over the globe. She felt a familiar gloom pushing
up from under her thoughts as it always did when she
considered the fragmentation of her life. She pushed it down
again and fixed her attention on the present moment. It was
time for lunch. 'I'll get some sandwiches,' she said to her
mother, who nodded and remained where she was.

The next day she drove back to New York. It had been a
good visit, and she had, eventually, told her mother about
Edward. Her mother had seemed to be rather amused. Gillian
had broached the subject at dinner, after their second glass of
wine. She had no talent for oblique attack. 'Well, Mother,' she
had said, 'I have something interesting to tell you. I'm in love.'

'Really, darling? With whom?' Her mother's eyes sparkled
with a sudden interest in the present.

'Oh, you should be pleased, you with your insatiable
appetite for crime novels. His name is Edward Gisborne, and
he's a Scotland Yard detective.'

'If you think I'll be shocked, you'll be disappointed,' her mother said placidly.

'Oh, Mother. I gave up trying to shock you when I was sixteen.'

'Did you, darling? I hadn't realized. Well, tell me about your detective. It sounds rather unlikely.'

'Yes, doesn't it. He's my age; he lives in London, he's shrewd and witty. He says he's a realist, which means he's conservative. And he looks like an Italian football player (soccer to you, Mother) masquerading as a banker.'

'Well. He doesn't sound much like Roderick Alleyn.'

Gillian giggled. 'No. I can't say he is. Oh, Mother, would you have liked me to bring home an aristocratic sleuth?'

'Are you going to bring him home?'

Gillian stopped laughing. 'I doubt it.' She paused. 'Life doesn't seem to be that...malleable.'

'Oh dear. Is he married?' Her mother was disconcertingly practical at times.

'No. He was once, years ago.'

'Well, darling, if he's not married, and he still has his teeth, what is the problem?'

'It's complicated.'

Her mother threw up her hands. 'In my day, love was not complicated. What a mess you children make of it.'

'Are you going to proffer the wisdom of the ancients now?' asked Gillian, laughing but vexed.

'No. It wouldn't be a particle of use. But I am curious. How in the world did you meet him?'

'It was two years ago. I was in London that summer and a woman I'd known in Vancouver was killed in England. I told you about that, remember?'

'Of course. But you didn't tell me you'd fallen in love.'

'No. Well, I had to go back to Vancouver, and how was I to know it wouldn't all evaporate?'

'I see. And it hasn't. What are you going to do about it?'

'God knows.'

'You'd like living in London—'

'Yes, but I don't have a job there. I can't just move there and be a wife. Besides, I'm not sure he's capable of living with anybody. He's been on his own for years, and he's completely unaccustomed to considering anything on the same plane as his work, which, I may add, does not mesh easily with a personal life. And we haven't really had enough time together.'

Her mother sighed. She picked up her glass, and the deep red wine glowed in her hand. 'Enjoy your year, darling. But I wish you would bring him home. I would enjoy meeting a real Scotland Yard detective.'

Gillian's flight to London left late the next day. She went in a lighthearted mood, filled with anticipation. It would be a year of work uninterrupted by teaching and administrative duties, a year in London, a year with Catherine, her closest friend, and most of all a year with Edward. If the airplane did not fall into the sea, she thought, she would be there in a few hours. The airplane did not fall, and London was there, waiting for her, in its sprawling, tarnished splendour. She immersed herself instantly; it was a world she knew well.

And now, here she was in Cambridge once more, after such an interval of years. It had been a perfect world when she was a student, and it had still the power to draw her, with its beauty and its distilled intensity. But its rarefied air changed those who breathed it. She was not certain that, in Cambridge, she would remain herself.

CHAPTER 11

Gillian spent the rest of the afternoon in the University Library, resolutely ignoring the world. Various other people there were doing the same and looked as though they did it all the time. At the end of the day she went back to Bee's house, where Edward telephoned her to say that he would join her for dinner if Basil and his wife were still prepared to receive him.

Edward was tired, and he needed some decent food, an elusive commodity in Cambridge restaurants. He would not be deserting his post, because he expected an evening with Basil Peters to be informative, not merely pleasant. He offered to pick Gillian up at 7:00, intending to save her a long walk in the dark (police work had developed his protective instincts) and make a quick, unofficial inspection of the Bee-Toby menage. So far, the evidence they had found pointed to only one possible conclusion: that Fiona Clay had killed Alistair Greenwood. The gun in her handbag had been covered with prints—hers, Greenwood's and Pamela's, but some of Fiona's prints were superimposed on the others. She had handled the gun after they had, that is, after Greenwood had locked it away. Superintendent Hardy was satisfied, though he admitted that it would be nice to find one person who had seen her in Cambridge on Monday, and he agreed with Edward that there were still too many loose ends lying about. Edward was less inclined to ignore alternatives, at least until he discovered how she had retrieved the gun. Perhaps someone had helped her—a far-fetched idea, but still one that merited consideration. And there were other things he wanted to know. Right now, dozens of policemen were on the job, checking trains and buses, circulating a description of Fiona, and making inquiries in pubs all over Cambridge. Meanwhile, it would not hurt to follow parallel lines of investigation while they were fresh, and while others were excavating Fiona Clay's interesting life in London.

Edward arrived late, and Gillian took him into the bleak sitting-room, where she was having a drink with her hosts. Toby was on the verge of departure, and he was rather smartly dressed. One of the college's former students—a rich American—had been invited to dine at high table. 'All Americans are rich, of course,' Toby was remarking breezily as Edward entered, 'But this one positively wallows in wealth.' He paused momentarily to offer Edward a drink, which Edward declined, and then clattered on at high speed, fumbling for a cigarette. 'Comes from one of those Jewish dynasties that are always building public monuments to house their art collections, or founding educational institutions. And a good thing, too. We can't allow all that excess money to go to waste buying political parties and football teams. We must hope that this latter-day Croesus will pour money over us like a jug of cream.'

'What will you tempt him with?' Gillian inquired. 'His name in letters of gold on the new chapel roof?'

'No, no, my dear. On the library. Just his line, and we desperately need an extension to house the Baddingsley bequest. It's only a thousand books, or so, but they can't be squeezed in just anywhere. They must be kept together, according to the terms of the bequest, and in suitable conditions. In other words, temperature and humidity control. Not to mention security. It's a natural history collection, volumes and volumes—beautifully preserved, of course—of the most exquisite illustrations. Such a temptation to thieves, when they can turn a tidy profit merely by stealing one book and cutting it up, selling off the pages one by one—'

'Quite,' said Edward. 'And the libraries, particularly at the universities, seldom do enough to protect themselves. There have been some appalling instances recently. I seem to recall an enormous Audubon folio in one case—the young man simply walked out of the college library carrying it under his arm.' The comment, a tacit reminder of Edward's profession, was coldly received.

'Yes, that's how it would appear to you, of course. But the point is, security is distasteful. Cameras and God knows what—a frightful business. A library ought to be a civilized place.' Toby shrugged. 'However, I don't suppose our guest and possible benefactor will object. Americans don't seem to mind bits of machinery hanging about.'

'Yes, well, American machinery usually works,' Gillian retorted. 'When *your* thief arrives, the camera shutter will be stuck, and you'll be waiting two months for a replacement part, you will have shut off the electronic gismo at the door because it buzzed constantly and at random, like all those deafening burglar alarms in London, and the technician who was supposed to have fixed it will be having a tea break.'

Toby, who seemed to be in an even more waspishly nervous humour than usual, began to reply. Gillian talked faster. 'But all will be saved,' she continued remorselessly, a fit of irresponsibility getting the better of her, 'by old Professor Herbivore, who, sidling myopically down the corridor in search of a lost Latin misquotation, will seize the miscreant and immobilize him with a discourse on Cicero until lunch-time.'

'At which point,' added Bee, who liked this turn of the conversation because it seemed to be annoying her husband, 'the technician will return—but only to collect his tools and go home.'

Toby waved his cigarette at them dismissively. 'Since the extension to the library is at present merely imaginary, I don't propose to debate the merits of its possible security arrangements with you. Perhaps we'll have eunuchs to guard it,' he finished, regretting this additional flourish instantly, but too late.

Bee smiled, showing her large, healthy teeth. 'Why, yes. The very thing,' she said sweetly. 'One sees so many of them about the old place, and they're obviously in need of something to do.'

She poured herself another drink, offering one to Gillian, who refused, thinking that it was about time she and Edward left. Edward gave Toby an amiable smile. 'But it would seem that the—er—Baddingsley bequest is something of a burdensome gift. Are you frequently offered, and do you often accept, gifts that entail immense additional expense to yourselves?'

'No, not really. Such offers are not all that common. And a rich college would have far less difficulty finding suitable accommodation for a collection of rare books. We, however, are among the impecunious colleges, so we have to scrape around. We'll manage, one way or another; a superb collection like Baddingsley's cannot be turned away.'

'But how impecunious are you?' Gillian asked curiously. 'Everyone knows that Trinity is terribly rich and some of the others are well off too, but do any of the colleges actually have to worry about money? Or are they merely poor, as, say, the man who can only afford one race horse is poorer than the man who owns a string of them?'

'I find your analogy inappropriate,' Toby replied, 'but we're not desperate. We do not wonder at the end of each fiscal year whether there will be another. However,' he continued, becoming authoritative and crisp, like a politician in an uneasy interview who by chance is asked a question he wants to answer, 'Cambridge is trying to preserve a special and extremely expensive system. I wouldn't care to advocate it as an efficient way to educate the millions, but it's a superb way to educate the few. Enough of them deserve it and will go on to justify it.' He stabbed his cigarette at the ashtray. 'And then, we've been around for rather a long time, you know. Tradition is worth something, I think. It would be a terrible pity if seven centuries of scholarly life were to come to an end through some pedestrian conception of thrift.'

'But is tradition always a good thing? Isn't it a dead weight, sometimes?' asked Edward.

'If only it were. No, it's a feeble counterbalance to the hysterical lust for change that infects this society. The American sickness.'

Gillian cringed. This was atrocious, even for Toby.

'Lust of any kind is a rare jewel in these parts,' said Bee, who also seemed edgier than usual.

Gillian caught Edward's eye. Time to go, unless he wanted to witness a row. She set down her empty glass. 'Right now, I have an almost hysterical lust for Elizabeth's food. And we should be on our way or we'll be late.' They escaped into the cool, damp October evening. Fog hung in the still air. Gillian was thankful that they were having dinner with Basil and Elizabeth. Edward had seen Toby at his very worst, and she quite urgently wanted him to see a contrasting side of Cambridge. She wondered whether he would make some excoriating remark. He took a detached view of human nature; he had to, in his job. On occasion, however, his comments were blistering.

But he said mildly, 'The college is Toby's whole life, isn't it? And there must be others like him here.'

'Oh yes. Bachelors who live in college—and bachelors who happen to be married.'

'Toby is married to his college, I'd say. No wonder his wife hates Cambridge.'

'Whoa. You're right about Toby, but wrong about Bee. Toby's a side-show in Bee's war with Cambridge.'

'What exactly is it, then? Why does every remark of hers shoot out like a poisoned dart?'

'History. Bee got her Ph.D. in the nineteen-sixties, when I did. Posts for women were even scarcer than they are now. She was good, but Cambridge jobs—for women—went only to the very best. And yet men who were not as good scholars as she was did get jobs, because there were more openings for them. But she wanted so badly to be here that she stuck around, publishing articles—which takes a hell of a lot of discipline when you're on your own—making a bare living at tutoring and supervisions and hoping the system would open up and give her a chance. It hasn't. She's a good academic living without recognition and without money. Naturally she's bitter. As for Toby, he's part of the status quo, which she can't forgive, and I would guess that she hates herself for living partly off his salary—his immoral earnings, as it were. Sorry—I didn't mean to give you a lecture. I'm upset by the effect this place has had on her.'

'Why doesn't she leave Cambridge?'

'Because she's not ready to admit defeat.'

Edward was silent for a moment. Then he asked: 'And what about Toby? What was he like when he was younger?'

'Before he fossilized? I didn't know him well. He was very intense—but he was charming, too. And he had enough marrow to attract a woman like Bee.'

'He seems pretty brittle now.'

They were crossing the fen, driving over the causeway in the misty darkness. Before them, the trees were dimly outlined against the glow of the town, but the stars were invisible.

'No one mentioned Alistair Greenwood,' Gillian remarked. 'Or Fiona Clay. They couldn't talk about anything else before you arrived.'

'That's not unusual. My job makes people reticent. It's partly courtesy and not wanting to appear vulgarly inquisitive, and it's partly fear.'

'Something was certainly eating at Toby tonight. And you made him nervous.'

'I thought so too,' said Edward. 'And I wonder why.'

CHAPTER 12

A few minutes later, Gillian rang Basil Peters' doorbell. She waited on the step, in the pale, metallic light cast by the street lamps, while Edward stood a little below and behind her, looking up and down the quiet row of houses half-hidden within their small but luxuriant gardens.

Melbourne Place was attractive and conveniently central; its short, narrow length ran east away from Parker's Piece, meeting at its far end a small street containing less comfortable housing and several pubs. Basil opened the door wide, and bright, golden light spilled over them. They went in, and Gillian felt herself relaxing. Basil and Elizabeth had been kind to her fifteen years earlier, and they would be the same now. They were not the sort of people who withered. Basil had always remained a little remote, never touching upon personal matters, but Elizabeth, buoyant with hospitable interest, floated over the barriers. Approaching her, the ego's claws gently retracted. Yet she was not uncritical of the varied specimens of humanity that passed through her hands—almost literally through her hands in many instances, she being a GP with a busy practice—she had crisp opinions. These were, however, anchored in kindness, and that gave them an authority which waspish pronouncements, even elegantly phrased, could not sustain.

She appeared at the top of the stairs, just a middle-aged woman in a Liberty print dress until her smile, like a shaft of light, revealed the vivid person. Basil led the way up to her. Like them, their house was upper-middle, solid, secure, and extremely comfortable. It had been furnished with unforced, muted good taste; to Gillian, it was an undemanding, padded sort of environment. It lacked individuality, although they did not. Gillian thought of Greenwood's superb, uncomfortable house, and wondered what sort of mental notes Edward was making. Being what he was, he had an acute eye for detail; being English, he used it to classify his fellow countrymen. In Gillian's experience, the English did it automatically the minute they met. She regarded this ineradicable habit with dismayed fascination and amid the skirmishing thanked her stars that she was North American and thus had noncombatant status. Each time she went to England, however, she would catch herself watching and classifying too; the English disease was highly infectious, and she took a secret, guilty pleasure in learning the clues of custom and language that revealed to the English the hideous secrets of each other's origins. After a while, trying not to do it was like trying not to think of the word rhinoceros. Edward said the class system was an idiotic anachronism, but he couldn't help knowing where he fitted in. 'I'm a rare sub-species,' he had once told Gillian. 'I'm an upper-class street urchin.' It had been an unusual, luxurious Sunday; they had been lying in Edward's bed, the papers strewn around, the coffee cups empty, the telephone miraculously silent. A warm square of sunshine crept across the bedclothes. Edward sighed a relaxed little sigh and put both arms round Gillian. 'My parents loathed the country and never went near it,' he went on. 'My father said it was always cold and frightfully boring, and my mother said she got palpitations if she travelled too far from Harrod's. She still says it, in fact. I think she believes marching through Harrod's is good for her health. She's religious about it the way some people are religious about running.'

'But if your parents were like that, where did you get your tough-as-old-boots, self-constructed quality?'

'Sheer neglect. And knocking about London, I suppose. My father was at Eton and hated every minute of it, so oddly enough he didn't send me there. I stayed in London and went to the local grammar school. But that didn't mean that my parents wanted me underfoot. They paid no attention to me. I played truant and spent my time on the streets. I learned everything I know about London then, and it's proved invaluable at the Yard. I played a lot of football, too, and I had an insatiable appetite for films. Movies, that is. I picked up as many Americanisms as I could, because they irritated my father.'

'Is that why you picked me up?'

'Who picked up whom?'

'You asked me to dinner.'

'So I did. It was most irregular. But you seemed tough, too—I liked that. And you were just in London for a holiday; there wasn't time to be diffident and English about it.'

This scene passed rapidly through Gillian's mind as she mounted the stairs in Basil's house. There hadn't been many occasions as sweet and carefree as that unburdened Sunday. Edward had gone on talking; he had even spoken briefly about his marriage, which had lasted for four years, about two years longer than it had lived. As it decomposed, he had disappeared into his work, pouring himself into it until there was nothing left over. He was habituated now; he had constructed a life and was reluctant to jeopardize it, to lift the stone and disturb what lay beneath. Yet it was precisely for this that he sought Gillian out: the lifting and the disturbance.

That was the most Edward had ever told her about himself, and then she hadn't seen him again for more than a week. He sought her out, and he retreated. Yet now he was in Cambridge: he had actually left London to see her. It was the bitterest of jokes that he had arrived only to have a murder happen under his nose. She wondered what the evening with Basil and Elizabeth held in store; Edward had professional reasons for coming, and she would hear in her imagination the hiss of a tape-recorder intruding upon the conversation.

Upstairs in the sitting-room, a small fire was burning gaily. Long curtains shut out the night, and a tray of bottles and glasses was set out. A fitted carpet covered the floor, an upholstered sofa and several armchairs filled the centre of the room, and various lamps shed a bright, cosy light on the room's tones of cream and grey. On the walls hung a few reticent prints.

Gillian sank into a chair and accepted a drink, sitting back while Basil, in a leisurely, oblique fashion, set about finding out who Edward might be. It was an interesting process. They were both old hands at interrogation, in their different spheres, and both were shrewd, and guarded, and deft. Moreover, Edward was accustomed to being a bit of a curiosity. She watched contentedly while Elizabeth disappeared into the kitchen.

Elizabeth's dinners were plain but good, the sort of food that provided a natural obbligato to conversation, distracting neither by failing to please nor by demanding attention. There was spinach soup, and then English lamb with roast potatoes and green beans, followed by a leafy salad, an extravagant, luscious trifle, and a large chunk of Stilton from the cheese stall in the market. The talk sailed easily over familiar political, economic and literary waters, but returned to Cambridge with a frequency that surprised Gillian. She eyed Edward speculatively now and then. Was Cambridge such an insular world, or was he steering the conversation that way, for his own reasons?

Elizabeth asked Edward whether he had been in Cambridge before.

'No, never. I hardly ever leave London. Rural pleasures have no allure for me.'

'Cambridge isn't exactly rural!'

'Yes, I know. But I'm blinkered. Anywhere past Epping Forest is the back of beyond to me.'

His insouciance permitted Elizabeth's next question. 'You didn't even think of being a student here?'

'No. I went to the University of London,' Edward said cheerfully. 'It never occurred to me to leave London and go to some little city to educate myself.'

Elizabeth was not an habitual fencer, and Gillian wondered what she had made of Edward's reply. It was a textbook English answer, perfectly balanced between the plausible and the amusing. Gillian had had much experience of this kind of answer, and she knew how it worked: like a sort of conversational lob, it dropped slowly and harmlessly down yet circumscribed the possible responses with wondrous effectiveness. It was a perfect defensive weapon, and the English were amazingly good at using it; they could keep it up for hours. Greenwood had been a grand master of this technique, and also of the oblique response, which, like a passing shot, skimmed by the question just out of reach. Still, he had differed from the multitudes who practised the art of disembodied conversation around the dinner tables of England. In his hands even defensive weapons had been forms of attack.

Edward, however, was merely keeping his distance. She was entertained by his skill, which showed to advantage in Cambridge, where this upper-middle-class art form reached its apogee among a concentration of the educated all practising it upon each other. He would do very well at high table. On the other hand, she regretted that he was so guarded; it was unnecessary in this house.

Gillian picked up the thread of the conversation. Retreating in good order, Elizabeth offered a generalization about who did choose Cambridge and why, and the conversation travelled smoothly from there to who did well at Cambridge and why, and from thence to the questionable value of examinations, a perennial topic at all academic institutions. At this juncture, Edward remarked casually, 'Gillian was telling me recently about an odd little device called an *aegrotat*. It sounded like a convenient loophole in the system. How does it work, exactly?'

Basil explained, something he enjoyed doing. 'I suppose it might sound a little offhand, but it's not, really. Each student receives quite a measure of attention here, you know. Between having a tutor, and attending weekly supervisions, he and his work are bound to be well known to someone. Given the system here, it's not all that difficult to assess with sufficient accuracy a student's chances in an examination. The mechanism, as it were, operates like this: if a candidate is absent from an examination—owing to illness, ordinarily— his tutor may, on his behalf, apply to the Standing Committee for Applications for an allowance. In fact, if the student becomes ill beforehand, the tutor may notify the Committee in advance that he is intending to apply. Then, when the student fails to appear for the examination, the tutor sends the application form to the Committee, and the Committee is empowered to instruct the Board of Examiners to make an allowance. When this is done, the student is deemed to have satisfied the examiners just as if he had been present at the examination. That's an *aegrotat*.'

Edward looked slightly puzzled. 'Does the Committee scrutinize the student's work?'

'Oh no. One committee handles the applications from all fields—from history to histology—so its members can hardly be expected to embrace the qualifications necessary to evaluate students in every discipline. Besides, there would be no time. There's a frightful load of work to get through before Degree Day. It's the tutor's function to know the student and to become sufficiently familiar with the general state of his work. Ordinarily, he would consult the student's Director of Studies before making the application for an allowance.'

'So the tutor recommends that the student be allowed to pass, and that's all there is to it?'

'More or less, leaving aside minor variations. Except for the medical certificate, of course. The student must provide proof that he was unfit.'

'A basic precaution,' said Edward. 'It sounds very sensible and simple, but isn't a device of this sort open to abuse?'

'Abuse? Sham illness, that sort of thing?'

'That sort of thing, yes.'

Basil shrugged. 'I suppose the occasional undeserving candidate slips through, a borderline case who is given the benefit of the doubt—or, in the old days,' he added with a glint of sarcasm, 'a cricket blue some college didn't care to lose. But I'm certain the instances are exceedingly rare. Certainly not frequent enough to warrant withdrawing such a useful and humane instrument. That would be to succumb to the bureaucratic disease.'

Edward murmured, 'I see,' and pursued the matter no further.

It was not until dinner was over that the subject of Greenwood's murder was allowed to surface, the others waiting for Edward to broach it. They had returned to the sitting-room, where the fire had died to a dull glow among the ashes. Gillian and Basil were drinking brandy; Elizabeth held a little glass of Cointreau from which she occasionally took a sip. Outside, a wind had risen and was rustling among the dying leaves. Elizabeth had asked Gillian what it felt like to come back after fifteen years.

'It's a queer sensation. Cambridge looks just the same, but I don't feel the same. When I was a student, it was as though I were living inside a dream. Now I'm outside it. It seems a bit unreal—but then I feel oddly insubstantial myself. Like Wordsworth: "I was the dreamer, they the dream."'

'You aren't about to say that Cambridge isn't the real world, are you?' Elizabeth said fiercely. 'I am *so* tired of hearing that. From my perspective as a GP, Cambridge is as real as any other place. People suffer from illness and disappointment and sorrow, they work hard, they have jobs and children and mortgages. And why does no one remember that there is an entire town full of people who are not academics?'

'The architecture makes one forget. So do the memories. And the history—how can one feel ordinary walking through these courts knowing that Erasmus and Newton once walked those same pathways? And Marlowe and Milton—'

'Don't forget Byron. He kept a bear in his rooms,' remarked Basil.

'Besides, the *recherché* is cultivated here,' Gillian persisted. 'The legendary and the eccentric are preserved, along with the rituals of another age. And you can't deny that there are many for whom Cambridge *is* a refuge from the twentieth century.'

'But that isn't what's important. What matters is the work that is done.'

'I know that. But the image matters as well. People who aren't connected to the work don't see it; they see, well, they see a refinement of oddity.'

'Gillian's right,' said Basil. 'Cambridge is an icon—and not just to outsiders. That's why Londoners are always saying it isn't the real world.'

'But what do they *mean*?' asked Elizabeth. She turned to Edward. 'What do you think? As a London policeman, you should have the qualifications to define reality.'

Edward looked at Gillian with dismay. 'Do they always ask questions like that at Cambridge dinner parties?'

'Sure. There's a list of ten questions. Defining reality is the easy one.'

'Let's give Edward an *aegrotat*,' said Basil. 'Elizabeth, you know what they mean: that Cambridge is isolated and beautiful. And that academics don't do anything useful.'

'I think it has a lot to do with high table,' said Elizabeth. 'More that than the buildings.'

'Those old college walls do seem to shut out the world,' Gillian replied.

'But they don't, do they?' Edward said. 'They didn't keep Alistair Greenwood safe.'

A silence followed, compounded of respect for the dead and tacit agreement that Edward should direct this portion of the conversation. He continued: 'If I may presume upon your hospitality, I'd like to ask you about Professor Greenwood.'

'We'll help in any way we can,' said Basil, turning to Elizabeth, who nodded vigorously in assent.

'Thank you,' Edward said formally. 'You know, of course, that Greenwood was shot yesterday. You may also be aware that a young woman called Fiona Clay was found dead in the Cam this morning, and that she, like Gillian, was a guest at Greenwood's house on Sunday. The conclusion that the two deaths are connected is virtually inescapable, but we haven't yet established the nature of the link.'

'Yes, we heard about Miss Clay,' said Basil.

Edward looked at him. 'You must have known Alistair Greenwood for a long time. Will you tell me what sort of a man he was?'

Basil leaned back in his chair and sucked meditatively at his pipe. In a more self-conscious man, it might have been a contrived pause, the pompous gesture of one too used to instructing the less enlightened. But Basil was merely arranging his thoughts. 'I've known him for nearly thirty years, and I'll be glad to tell you what I can. You're bound to hear much that's unbalanced. The most significant thing about Alistair Greenwood is that he was a great scholar. So far as history is concerned, nothing else matters. And although history is not what concerns you now, Greenwood's scholarly pre-eminence isn't something you can afford to ignore, because he lived the part: he saw himself as a great man and scholarship as a high calling. He was, I'm afraid, arrogant, patrician, isolated and deeply disdainful of society—a sump of foolishness and corruption.'

'Was he something of a recluse, then?' asked Edward.

'Not really. He bore his part in college life—dinners, sherry parties, receptions for visiting scholars and so on. He often had people to Sunday lunch. But he had few friends—few people he would see informally just for the sake of their company. Most of humanity bored him.'

'Family?'

Basil smiled. 'Everyone has one, I suppose. He observed the conventional ties—'

'You mean the way some people go to church at Christmas and Easter,' broke in Elizabeth.

'Perhaps. I never heard him speak affectionately of his relations.'

'No—er—romantic interests?' said Edward.

'I wouldn't know,' replied Basil. 'What do you think, Elizabeth?'

'I shouldn't think so. But one never knows. The most surprising feelings are hidden inside people. I've seen some of my patients for years and years, but they still come out with things that simply amaze me.'

'He always seemed solitary to me,' put in Gillian. 'I wonder what price he paid for being a Cambridge legend.'

'Perhaps his life,' Elizabeth replied.

Edward shot her a quick glance. 'What do you mean?'

'That he was a symbol as well as a man. And symbols can inspire insane behaviour.'

Edward turned back to Basil. 'What drove him to be an historian? Why not a mathematician—a scientist? If he loathed humanity, why did he immerse himself in its long, sad story?'

'His training was classical and his gifts were literary. And he found solace in the past, solace and companionship. Perhaps even redemption. One cannot be an historian without hope.'

A sombre silence descended, as if the fact of Greenwood's death, which had wheeled above them all evening, its shadow moving from face to face or darkening the room, had with Basil's words plummeted suddenly and settled in their midst.

Later, as Edward was driving Gillian back to Newnham, he said, 'I've been to see Cooper-Hewson. His name was on Greenwood's desk, you recall.'

'Greenwood was going to ask him about Wing's *aegrotat*.'

'Right. Well, I asked what sort of a student Wing was. I can't say he told me very much, but then I wasn't telling him much, either. However, I did learn two things: first, Wing was neither brilliant nor diligent. He treated Cambridge as a playground—was always larking about, as my parents' generation would have said—and didn't do his work. He would have had trouble passing his exams. Second, Toby Fox was his tutor.'

'I see. And what did Cooper-Hewson think about the *aegrotat*?'

'He hadn't been aware that Wing had been given one. I'd say he was disconcerted when I mentioned it.'

Gillian looked thoughtful. 'Tell me, is Wing from Hong Kong?'

'Clever girl. Of course he is.'

'Well. That's one of Sunday's mysteries cleared up, at least.'

'Perhaps more than one. Suppose Greenwood thought the *aegrotat* was fishy, and suppose he was right. Then what?'

'If a formal investigation reached that conclusion, Wing would lose his degree, and I guess Toby could lose his job. Maybe not—but his career and his reputation would be ruined.'

'That could pass as a motive for Toby Fox.'

'Maybe. But why would he take such a risk for Wing?'

'I don't know.' He did not add that he hoped Wing was about to tell him. Wing had a plummy job at a bank in London, and Jagger, a colleague of Edward's at the Yard, was going to pay him an unexpected visit the next day. The word murder usually made people nervous, they were apt to tell one all sorts of things.

CHAPTER 13

Edward drove back to the police station. He was wide awake again and anxious to push on with the case, and he thought his nets might have some new fish in them. He was not disappointed. The Yard had been busy and had sent on the results of an interview with Greenwood's London solicitor. Edward tore open the envelope with a certain wolfish anticipation; Greenwood's will was bound to be interesting. He was pleased that the report came from Jagger, who was always thorough and possessed an unassuming talent for organizing information.

Not unexpectedly, Greenwood had left a considerable estate. There was the house, with its land and choice furnishings, and then there were the Rolls, a nice chunk of invested income and his royalties. Edward looked to see where these windfalls would land. The first name on the list was Mary Greenwood Forbes. That was the sister, Edward knew. According to Pamela Ditton, she had married an impover-ished landowner in the Orkneys, and the family had hardly seen her since. 'She lives in a freezing ruin and has aban-doned the South and all its spurious luxury.' Greenwood had left her the Rolls-Royce. Edward smiled a little and read on, anxious to discover what Denham might receive. But if Denham's fortunes were failing, they would continue to do so. Denham got the contents of the wine cellar, nothing more.

Doubtless it was a good cellar, Edward thought, but he didn't fancy oenophilia as a motive for murder.

Pamela Ditton's name came next; Greenwood had left her the Stubbs Edward had seen in the dining-room at Camford House. Edward whistled. A few hundred thousand pounds' worth of canvas was quite a nice legacy for Cousin Pamela. And it was a lovely Stubbs, too. What was it Pamela had said on Sunday? He leafed through Gillian's statement. 'She might have missed Alistair and put a hole in the Stubbs.' That was suggestive, but then where did it lead?

Below Pamela's name, Jagger had listed the housekeeper, Mrs. Hill. She received £500. That was unexceptional, but Jagger was having his fun, leaving the house until last. Edward didn't mind, he had known Jagger for too many years, and, besides, he was enjoying himself. He liked wills—they were full of strange meat.

The house was there, preceded by the royalties, which were left to Trinity College, to be used for the benefit of the Wren Library. The bulk of the estate, the property, the house and its contents, and the invested income, were bequeathed to King's College, where Greenwood had been a student.

As Edward studied the terms of the bequest, he wondered how delighted King's would be. The income was to be used for the acquisition of books and to maintain the property, which could neither be sold nor altered. In other words, thought Edward, Greenwood had proffered his library in return for a bell-jar. And it must be a damned good library, for it was a legacy that was likely to be burdensome—like the Baddingsley bequest. But then a library that could be lived in was doubtless, for some, an approximation of paradise.

There was a tap on the door, and Detective Chief Superintendent Hardy stuck his head in. 'There's a wire for you from Hong Kong.'

'Good. Come in and look at this. It's a summary of Greenwood's will.'

Hardy glanced through it. 'He's left the crumbs to the family—big crumbs, mind you—and the loaf to the college.'

'Yes. Family feeling seems to have run a little thin in his veins. Does anything else strike you?'

'The wine. Didn't Gillian Adams state that the wine was Denham's? That he'd given it to his brother? You could say that giving it back was a cute way of giving him nothing.'

'Then I wish he'd left that particular version of nothing to me. But I agree, and that's how I'd interpret it, given what I've learned of his character. There's something about Pamela's Stubbs that bothers me too, but I can't quite place what it is.' Edward had been fiddling with a plastic spoon. A piece snapped off and fell into a cup of cold coffee.

'You've been up too long,' said Hardy. 'And I'm knackered. Why not come home with me and have a whisky? We can put you up.'

'Another time, if I may, thanks all the same. If I try to go to bed now, my mind will keep buzzing like a fly in a box. Have you got that wire?'

'Here it is.' Hardy had stuffed it absent-mindedly into his pocket; now he took it out and uncrumpled it.

'Well, well, well,' Edward said after reading through it. 'Wing's daddy is a very big daddy. Perhaps the light begins to dawn.'

'It's still midnight in my time zone.'

'Then go home to bed. I'll refrain from inflicting my latest brilliant theory upon you until tomorrow.'

Hardy left. Edward leaned back in his chair, put his feet on the desk and closed his eyes. Tomorrow he would see the ballistics reports and the PM on Fiona Clay, and he would hear from Jagger during the morning. Right now, he wanted to sort out the geography of the case: who was where at the crucial times.

First, Alistair Greenwood. He had gone out Sunday evening to visit a colleague, who had told Hardy that Greenwood had come at about nine o'clock and remained until nearly midnight. Greenwood had mentioned the lunch but had not referred to anything out of the ordinary, and he had said he'd sat down to work as soon as everyone left, trying to finish drafting an article before going out. At midnight, he'd left, presumably to go home to bed. He'd remained at home all morning on Monday. The housekeeper, Mrs. Hill, said she had cooked lunch for him, and he'd gone off to the university at about 1:30. This tallied with the information from the porters, who had seen him come through the college gate and ask for his letters at 1:45. He'd gone up to his rooms and had stayed there for at least part of the afternoon, for several telephone calls had been put through. He'd been seen leaving the college at 3:30, and at 4:00 he'd arrived at the Chetwynd Room.

Edward thought this over. Hardy was tracing Greenwood's activities, and it would not be long before they discovered where he had been between 3:30 and 4:00. Otherwise, there was no mystery about his behaviour, unless he hadn't gone home to bed Sunday night. Just now, the object was to find out when the keys might have been taken and the gun removed from the drawer. Not on Monday, Edward felt sure. Greenwood had been at home all morning, and Mrs. Hill had been there from 11:00 until 6:00. Moreover, her husband had come as well, to do a bit of gardening in the afternoon. He had been mowing the lawn in front of the house until nearly 4:00. Two people, one inside, one out, could scarcely have afforded the most resolute of intruders a safe opportunity to enter the house and take the gun. That left Sunday, when Greenwood was out or asleep. If he hadn't taken his key-ring, and he probably hadn't, since it was cumbersome, and an extra set of keys to the Rolls and the front door had been found in the pocket of the coat he had worn that evening, someone could have entered the house while he was gone, found the keys and removed the gun.

Who had had the opportunity to do so? Edward leafed through the rest of the statements. Victor Smallbone had visited acquaintances in Trinity during the evening and had attended a party after that. On Monday he had been busy as well, although the details were of little interest. Unlike the other academic lives Edward was inspecting, Victor's was relentlessly sociable. Breakfast with X, luncheon with Y, and then the drive back to Norwich at tea-time. He'd gone out again that evening at 10:00. According to his statement, he'd arrived in Norwich at 7:00, having had trouble with his car on the way, but Smallbone could produce no witnesses to confirm this. So, Edward concluded, it was possible that Smallbone had returned to Greenwood's house after leaving the party Sunday night, had shot Greenwood Monday afternoon and later driven coolly off to Norwich. But why? He had been a student of Greenwood's—doubtless a gruelling experience—and, according to Pamela, Greenwood had made it clear that he would prevent Smallbone from obtaining the coveted position at Cambridge. Was that enough? Edward thought not, but he knew very little about Smallbone. Perhaps Greenwood filled his narrow horizon, blotting out the light: obstacle, destroyer, impossible example. In that case—

He could pursue the subject no further at the moment, and he turned his attention to the remaining guests, of which there were five, excluding Gillian. He was becoming weary and confined his thoughts to the facts. Toby and Bee had been with Gillian until 10:00, when she had gone to bed, but they were each other's only alibi after that. And neither of them had an alibi for the time of Greenwood's death or the hours following it; each had been alone, working.

Pamela Ditton stood in much the same case. She had been alone all Sunday evening, having lied to Greenwood about going out that evening in order to excuse her early departure after lunch. On Monday, she had given a lecture in the morning and had spent the afternoon in the university library, she said. She couldn't think of anyone who had noticed her there. At 7:30 she'd gone into hall for dinner. She'd remained in the combination room until about 10:00 and had then returned alone to her rooms.

Edward looked at these statements with irritation. All this hard, solitary, academic work was commendable, no doubt, but it made it difficult to pin people down. He turned with something like relief to Denham's statement, which was full of times and places. He had unquestionably been in London Sunday evening, he had been in company and had spent the night with a woman—not Fiona Clay. Every minute of his time on Monday morning could be charted, from 6:00 when he started his working day until 3:00, or shortly before, when he left the office to go home and work alone. So far as Edward could see, he could not possibly have obtained the key and the gun. Nor was there anything suspicious about his alibi; Monday was typical of the way he spent his days, according to Jagger, who, thorough as usual, had checked.

There remained the problem of Fiona Clay. Where had she been between Sunday afternoon and Monday night? She had been seen in one of her local shops late Sunday afternoon, buying cigarettes, but that was all that had been discovered of her movements. She could have returned to Little Camford Sunday evening, but then where had she been all night? And the next day? And if she hadn't killed Greenwood herself and then tumbled into the river, to whom had she given the gun, and why? The more Edward thought about this angle, the less he liked it. He was stale, he acknowledged. It would be more profitable now to sleep than to think.

CHAPTER 14

The next day was Wednesday. Gillian planned to spend it wrapped in the industrious hush of the University Library. It was a cool, misty morning, and the green of the chestnut trees was tinged with gold. She gazed absently through the window of her little room in Bee's house and thought that what she would like to do would be to take Edward to Grantchester. They would walk along the path through the fields at noon, when the sun was high and the mists had risen from the river. There would be cows grazing in the wet meadows, and furrowed fields, brown and tidy after the autumn ploughing. Behind them, Cambridge would dwindle, until it was almost lost in the rural landscape. From the slight rise of ground near Grantchester, they would look back and see nothing but a fringe of trees and the towers pencilled on the hem of the sky.

They would walk into the village and then sit in the Green Man under the low ceiling with its desiccated beams, among the cosy litter of horse-brasses, and they would indulge in simple, non-cerebral pleasures. Edward was good at that, when he could be pried away from his work.

It occurred to her that she was seeing him in her own world for the first time. London was neutral territory, all big cities were, once one knew them well: they provided a variety of worlds from which to choose, and precious anonymity.

He had visited her once in Vancouver, but briefly, and they hadn't wasted their time acquainting him with the virtues of the university or making a tour of Gillian's friends when they hadn't seen each other for months.

Now here he was in Cambridge: not Gillian's native heath, but her sort of terrain. The juxtaposition filled her with pleasure and with an obscure sense of impending revelation.

She went downstairs. As she descended, she heard Bee rummaging and singing in a cracked contralto. 'Bee?' she said, astonished at this exhibition of good cheer. Bee was in the sitting-room, piling books into a motley collection of cardboard boxes from Sainsbury's.

'Get yourself a cup. I've made an enormous pot of coffee.' Gillian went to the kitchen and returned with a cup and warm slice of buttered bread. The coffee was hot, and the bread was delicious.

'It's the best bakery in Cambridge, except when he burns everything,' said Bee. She was moving energetically about the room, and dust motes swarmed so thickly that the shafts of light slanting through the bay window were an opaque gold.

'Have you decided to open a bookstall in the market?'

'No, but as it happens, I no longer have a problem finding space for these. I may as well tell you right now: I'm moving in with Pamela.'

'I thought she lived in rooms at King's.'

'She does. But she's looking for a house. There's one in Millington Road she has her eye on; it has a judas-tree in the front garden. Not that that's a reason to buy a house.' Bee was almost effervescent, her voice edged with defiance. 'Pamela is my lover, you see.'

'Is she? I see—I do see,' said Gillian, who saw some things that had puzzled her fall into place.

'Are you shocked?'

'Don't be silly.'

'I'm not. Lots of people will be.' Now Bee sounded faintly pleased.

'Does Toby know?'

'I told him last night. Pamela came to see me while he was dining in college and you were out with Edward, and we arranged it then. She'd suddenly made up her mind. She said she wanted to find a house and live in it with me. She wants some sort of life, she said, and she's never had one. Anyhow, I told Toby later when he came home. He made a frightful scene. God! What's the point? We'd already decided to get a divorce. He stormed out, and he hasn't been back since.'

'He didn't know until now?'

'Perhaps he didn't want to. And we were always terribly careful, not because of him, particularly, but Pamela didn't want anyone to know.' Bee dusted her hands and poured herself more coffee. The words rushed from her in a flood. 'Cambridge is a small world, though. I know there was some talk. Pamela was worried about it. We're still being discreet— I'm telling you because you're one of my oldest friends, and you're discreet, and anyhow you don't live here. Pamela's awfully private. I think we'll probably emerge gently from the closet in time, but not now. We'll move in together like two maiden aunts. That's an amazing leap for her—only two days ago—'

Bee stopped.

'What?' Gillian prompted, for Bee was momentarily lost in a painful recollection, and Gillian wanted this conversation to continue.

'Oh, I thought it was all over. God, I was depressed that night. However, it doesn't matter now,' she said briskly. 'What's bothering me—a bit—is Toby. I think he believes I'm doing all this just to make a fool of him. He doesn't understand at all. When Pamela found me, it was a sort of marvellous accident. I didn't plan any of it. But nothing will stop me now.'

She stood near the window, the swirling motes of dust making an aureole about her head, boxes of books, like tribute, piled about her feet. 'I can't wait to get out. Gillian— wish me luck. It's a new life.'

'I think you need one. And of course I wish you luck. But, well, I also wish you could consider leaving Cambridge, not just your husband.'

'You think it's warped me, don't you? Perhaps you're right. But I've grown to be the shape I am, and I don't feel as though I'd fit anywhere else. Besides—it will be different living with Pamela. It will transform the whole experience.'

Gillian looked at her as if across a shortening distance, as if she saw coming down a road a dim, nameless figure that in the space of a few steps became suddenly recognizable. This Bee—vigorous, full of conviction and expectation—was the Bee she remembered. 'You know,' Gillian said, 'I believe you.'

Bee stretched out her hand to the coffee-pot. For the first time since Gillian's arrival, they were at ease with each other.

While Gillian was having this illuminating conversation with Bee, Edward was talking to Scotland Yard. On the desk in front of him were the reports from Nottingham. The bullet that had killed Alistair Greenwood had come from the gun in Fiona Clay's handbag. And Fiona had died of drowning, sometime between 8:00 p.m. and midnight on Monday evening. Translating the prim language of the report, Edward noted that she must have been completely sozzled when she went into the river—undoubtedly drunk enough to have stumbled in her silly shoes, and quite possibly drunk enough to have passed out, as she had at lunch on Sunday. She could well have fallen into the Cam and drowned. But what was she doing by the river, and if she had drowned her sorrows after shooting Greenwood, where had she done it? The police had drawn a blank at all the local pubs and off-licences. Where had she been between Greenwood's death and her own?

Edward had also discovered when he read the report that she had taken some barbiturates within a couple of hours of her death and that the little bottle in her handbag contained traces of phenobarbital. This suggested a desire for oblivion, but Edward could not picture Fiona Clay sitting on a park bench drinking herself insensible. She must have been somewhere, and, he suspected, with someone.

Superintendent Hardy, while willing to listen to whatever Edward suggested, looked upon these complications with something less than enthusiasm. The fingerprints and the ballistics report linked Fiona indissolubly to Greenwood's death, and, although Hardy pressed on with a diligent and tedious search for witnesses who had seen her in Cambridge on Monday and eagerly awaited evidence from London of a previous connection to the Greenwoods, he was satisfied that she had done murder. Edward thought privately that if the Cambridge police were on their own they would close the case soon, whether or not they found any witnesses. It occurred to him that if there were a second murderer he (or she) had reason to regard Edward's unexpected presence in the Chetwynd Room as a piece of outrageously bad luck.

When Jagger telephoned from Scotland Yard, Edward mentioned this, making a grim joke of it. He passed on the news from Nottingham and asked what was new in London.

'Plenty,' was the reply. Jagger had been busy, and Edward scribbled furiously as he listened. As Edward had requested, Jagger had interviewed Mr. Wing. He had gone to the bank where Wing worked, in order to rattle him, and had not been gentle. 'It was as easy as opening a tin. I hinted that the police did not look kindly upon people who withheld evidence in cases of murder, and he dumped the whole story into my lap.'

'What did he say?'

'He told me his father had promised the college two hundred thousand pounds in exchange for his degree. He hadn't been doing very well, and at the beginning of his final year his father came over to see what could be done. And he cooked up this little scheme with Wing's tutor: Toby Fox. Fox promised to get Wing through somehow, and no one else knew anything about it. After Wing graduated in June, a gift was made to the college, but the quid pro quo remained secret.'

'I see. I presume the Master and the Bursar and various other people in the college know who gave the money but not why. There were no strings—visible strings—attached?'

'Correct. The donation was made to reward the college's "magnificent contributions to the culture of Britain and to support its invaluable role in the education of future leaders of Britain and the Commonwealth." And the donor requested anonymity. Nobody looked the gift horse in the mouth.'

'Hah!' said Edward with satisfaction. 'And why should they? All sorts of people give them money and books and bits of plate. And I'm sure they believe they do make a magnificent contribution.'

'How are you doing at your end, by the way? Getting anywhere, or are they all too smart for you?'

'I'd say the case is moving very quickly. There's nobody here who doesn't talk, for one thing. But I was requested to define reality last night. I wish you'd been there; I'd have liked to hear your answer to that one.'

'Hmph,' Jagger grunted. 'Who asked you that? Some philosopher? I'd have told him, "Why ask me? You're paid to think about that. I do my job, you do yours."'

'Actually, it was a doctor—a medical doctor.'

'A doctor? Christ! If anyone is neck-deep in reality every day, it's a doctor. Or does he just teach?' Jagger added suspiciously.

'No, she doesn't. And I gather she thinks policemen are neck-deep in reality.'

'Oh.' Jagger sounded mollified.

'What else have you got for me?'

'More on Fiona Clay. We've been digging. She's no rose, I can tell you. She's a model, or was. She made a nice packet at it for a while until her bad habits got in the way. Drugs and drink. She'd show up incapable or not show up at all. Her agency dumped her, eventually. They told me she'd acquired a pretty expensive cocaine habit by then. She seems to have found ways to keep herself supplied. She went to a lot of parties, always with rich men. Not an upmarket prostitute, exactly, but something fairly close to it.'

'Ah. A *demi-mondaine*. That's interesting.'

'What's that, when it's at home?'

'A woman of doubtful reputation, on the fringe of society. Dumas *Fils*. Look it up.'

'Piss off. Clay had some dubious friends, too. She was seeing one Rex Green, a nasty bit of goods. He kept her supplied with enough pills for a chemist's. He's dropped out of sight, but the gun she had must have belonged to him. The word is that he slept at her flat quite frequently, and the gun was there just in case anybody happened to pay him an unexpected visit.'

'Where was he between five and five-thirty on Monday?'

'Not in Cambridge, I regret to say. Right here in London, collecting from his bookmaker. Why does a thug like him win at five to one? When I go to the track it's like throwing money down a well.'

'I don't know. If I could answer that I could probably define reality. Anything else about Clay?'

'She was going to hell pretty fast. Sometimes she'd shut herself in her flat for days with her bottles and pills. Then she'd pull herself together and go out looking for someone to spend money on her.'

'Someone like Denham Greenwood.'

'Right. They did meet at that Chelsea party three weeks ago, so far as anyone knows, and he took her home. A model who used to see Clay now and then told us Clay had talked about him. He saw her several times before they went to Cambridge, and he spent his money freely. That's all we've got right now, but we're looking for Rex Green.'

'Anything on what she was doing between Sunday afternoon and Monday evening?'

'Not a dickey-bird. As I told you, she was seen in London on Sunday afternoon buying cigarettes. But after that, nothing. She was probably pouring gin down her throat in her own flat, but we can't prove it. There are half a dozen empty bottles of Gordon's in a box under the sink.'

'And you can't find any trace of an earlier connection to either of the Greenwoods?'

'Nothing has surfaced. What about your end?'

'I don't like it. It's suspiciously simple and convenient, and the gaps bother me. I don't think Fiona Clay acted alone. Someone else is involved.'

'Are you going to tell me who?'

'Not yet. But barring the mysterious bearded foreigner lurking in the stairwell, there are precious few possibilities. I should be able to eliminate one or two of them quite soon.'

'That's good. We can't leave you to swan around Cambridge indefinitely.'

Edward grinned into the telephone. 'Is the Superintendent riding you hard, old man?'

'Just let me know what else you need.'

'I will.'

'Right, then. *Sayonara.*'

'What?'

'*Sayonara.* It's Japanese for goodbye.'

'I know that. Why did you say it?'

'You'll find out when you come back,' Jagger replied, pleased with his own little mystery. 'Ta-ta.'

'Dammit,' Edward said to the dead telephone.

CHAPTER 15

He sat at his desk for a few minutes, contemplating what Jagger had told him. Outside, the common was still silvered with dew, and the evanescent blue of the sky was lost in a pearly haze near the horizon. He left word of his whereabouts with the front desk and went in search of Hardy. In the interests of good relations between the Yard and the local force, he was careful to pass on new information with the least possible delay.

Hardy's office was on the other side of the corridor; his windows commanded a view, not of grass and trees, but of parked cars and the grey wall of the security unit. Hardy, his back to this prospect, was making a chain of paper-clips. Steam curled upward from a battered blue cup in front of him.

'Like a nice cup of tea?'

Edward watched him drop six lumps of sugar into the thick, brown liquid. 'No, thanks all the same. But I would like a chat.'

'Good. I haven't talked to anybody this morning except my wife, and she's not pleased with me today.' He waved at some papers on his desk. 'By the way, we've found Dr. Temple for you—the chap who signed Wing's medical certificate. That is, we haven't found him. He's dead.'

'What!'

Hardy smiled. 'I got rather agitated too, when I heard that. But there's nothing in it. Natural causes. He died last month. Heart failure. He was semi-retired and had been ill off and on for the last few years.' He tapped the papers on his desk. 'It's all here.'

'But six months ago he examined Wing and signed the certificate?'

'He did. And he's been in and out of the college for years. He was a good friend of the previous Master's and used to come in to dine quite regularly even after the old Master died. A few years ago, he presented the college with a commemorative silver tankard. The old Master liked beer at lunch, seemingly, but not in a glass.'

'Dr. Temple was the perfect man for the job, I see.'

'But not much help to you now.'

'I don't think I need him. I've just had a report from Jagger in London.' Edward repeated what Jagger had told him about Wing.

Hardy sipped his tea. 'I have to admit, that's a nice motive: two hundred thousand pounds plus Fox's job and reputation. And Greenwood was after him in full cry. Between three-thirty and four on Monday he was digging out Wing's academic record.'

'Was he indeed? I wonder how he came to smell a rat.'

'He was chairman of the Board of Examiners. In history, of course. Maybe he investigated every *aegrotat* this year—just out of curiosity.'

'Or perhaps there were more of them than usual. As a good historian, he probably had a detective's nose for the unusual. What a piece of bad luck for Fox.'

'Just as you say. But where does Fiona Clay fit in?'

Edward leaned forward, suddenly intent. 'Think of her as a stalking-horse.'

'All right,' Hardy said. 'I'm listening.'

Edward passed on his new information. Then he said, 'Suppose that at that infamous lunch someone else who wanted Greenwood dead saw Fiona's display and in it an opportunity. She was a perfect patsy. Virtually everyone there hated Greenwood, and most of them had other reasons for wanting him out of the way. None of them has an alibi for Monday evening when Fiona Clay tumbled into the river. Fox, Ditton, Smallbone and Denham Greenwood are the cases we have to consider.'

'What about Fox's wife?'

'It's possible; she loathed the man. I'm not forgetting her, but why would she kill him, unless it was to protect her husband? And given that she loathes him too, and the system, that seems to be ruled out. So for the moment I'd prefer to leave her to one side.'

'And what about Gillian Adams? Friend of yours, isn't she?'

'That's right. But there are good reasons for eliminating her without dragging me in as a character witness. She didn't shoot Greenwood, and she couldn't have pushed Clay into the river. If you remember, she was at King's, and then with me, until she signed her statement and left the station at nine-forty-five. She took a taxi to Grantchester Meadows—that's been verified—and Bee Hamilton agrees that she arrived at ten. Toby Fox arrived about twenty minutes later. Unless you care to propose a conspiracy among all three of them...' Edward kept his tone neutral, suppressing his unprofessional resentment of the question.

Hardy nodded, at ease again. 'We'll leave it at that. Carry on.'

'Clay had her own reasons for feeling murderous; suppose one of our candidates offered her an additional incentive, such as money—she seemed to want it enough not to care how she got it—to return and finish the job. He retrieves the gun for her, tells her where to go, and when he meets her afterwards, instead of arranging to pay, or whatever, tidies away the evidence of his involvement by tidying her into the river. Take Fox. He could have gone back to Little Camford late Sunday evening after the two women were in bed. Maybe his wife has lied to us, or more likely she was sleeping off all that whisky and didn't hear him go. He leaves the gun somewhere for Clay, meets her after the deed is done, gives her a few stiff gins, supposedly to calm her down, and then— pop! she goes into the Cam.'

'But he—'

'Bear with me. Save the buts until the end. The same basic plot works for Ditton. She knew Greenwood's house and habits, and she has no alibi for Monday evening except during dinner.'

'Why would she want Greenwood killed?'

'He'd left her a Stubbs worth a quarter of a million pounds, and I think that those peculiar remarks of his on Sunday added up to a threat to change his will. She "stubbed her toe," he said. And Gillian said the comment made no sense except to Ditton, who became angry and upset. A few minutes later, he referred pointedly to Pamela's heirlooms.'

'He may have threatened to change his will every week. Some people enjoy that sort of thing. And given that we know of no reason for him to change it, your interpretation of a couple of simple remarks seems a trifle outlandish.'

'I don't think so. The more I learn about Alistair Greenwood, the more certain I am that it's the correct interpretation. There's probably something about Pamela Ditton we've missed.'

Hardy fidgeted with his paper-clips. 'He didn't like his family very much, or anyone else, for that matter. I'll give you that.'

'Then let's think about Denham.'

'He knew Clay. That should make him a front runner.'

'Just so. He knew her weaknesses better than the others did, and he arrived in Cambridge on Monday evening in plenty of time to dispose of her before coming here. He has money and a cool head; he likes a calculated risk. I don't yet know the state of his finances, but he may well have had great expectations of his brother's estate. The catch is, he was definitely in London all Sunday evening and all day Monday until three o'clock. So I don't see how he could have taken the gun.'

'And where was Clay all this time?'

'I don't know. But she must have gone somewhere after she bought the cigarettes. And she didn't use wings to get back to Cambridge.'

'All right. What about Smallbone?'

'Smallbone. Well, he has no alibi at the moment. He went to a party Sunday and left at one a.m., but he has a car and he can't prove that he went straight to bed. He says he was on his way to Norwich when Greenwood was killed, but he can't prove that either. No one saw him until ten in the evening. So it's just possible that he tipped Miss Clay into the Cam before he left Cambridge.'

Edward sat back and waited. Hardy sighed, a repressive, doleful sound. 'I agree with you that Clay scarcely seems competent enough to have managed the thing on her own, but, dammit, Gisborne, there are great bloody gaping holes in your theories. Victor Smallbone—what jury will ever believe he murdered two people for a job in Cambridge?'

'A jury of Bee Hamiltons would.'

'And as for the others, Fox doesn't have any money, Pamela Ditton's motive hangs on your interpretation of a couple of offhand remarks, and Denham was in London when you need him here.'

'Holes, yes. But the sort that can be patched. If one of these theories is the correct one, we'll sew it up. No. Those holes don't bother me particularly. What does disturb me is another question, one that applies to all the cases. What I want to know is, why was he killed at King's?'

'That's very queer—what's that expression? Queer as Dick's hatband? And if we knew why, we'd know who.' Hardy sighed again. 'But I don't know how to find the answer.'

'Nor do I. So let's get on with the usual. Fill in the holes.'

'Right. What do we want to know?' Hardy produced pencil and paper. 'One: did anybody see Smallbone and his car between here and Norwich on Monday? If so, when? I'd like to shorten our list. Two: any skeletons in Ditton's cupboard? That's your piece of the river, I'd say. Three: where was Fiona Clay before she drowned? On the tiles—but where?'

'They'll be working on that in London, too,' said Edward. 'I'd like to go and see for myself as soon as I can get away. That's enough to be going on with for the time being. Greenwood's funeral—it's this afternoon, isn't it?'

'That's right. Are you going?'

'I might. Something—or somebody—might turn up. And having witnessed Greenwood's death, I think I can pay my respects without causing offence. I shan't feel entirely like an FBI agent at a Mafia wedding.'

'Rather you than me,' said Hardy.

CHAPTER 16

Alistair Greenwood's funeral took place at the church in Little
Camford. Gillian arrived alone, driving Bee's car, Bee having
no need of it since she was to accompany Pamela. A few
people were already gathered in the churchyard; Gillian
recognized Greenwood's housekeeper, Mrs. Hill, and
surmised that the squat, bottle-nosed person beside her must
be her husband. They were talking with the vicar, a long bent
stick of a man with gnarled hands, lined, sunburnt skin, and
long, white hair raked thinly back over his pink skull.
Probably a serious gardener, Gillian thought. Cecil Corbett,
an historian at King's who had attended her lecture, was
standing further away in a patch of shade, looking too warm
in his dark suit. He was listening inattentively to a smaller
man whose back was oddly familiar. Gillian was briefly
puzzled, but then she saw his plump fingers flutter and
realized that it was Victor Smallbone.

What's he doing here, she thought. She would have
expected him to turn up at the memorial service in the college
chapel, an occasion of wider social opportunity. She did not
approach them, preferring to wait by herself in the shadow
of a great beech tree that spread its shapely branches over the
wall of the churchyard.

Hearing a car draw up, she turned and through a leafy
filigree glimpsed Pamela's Jaguar sedan. It stopped, but no
one got out immediately. Then the two women appeared,

patterns of dark fabric and pale skin moving in the sunlit road behind the green leaves. Car doors closed. Briefly, the two figures were still, visible between branches, Pamela leaning against the car, Bee close beside her. Gillian remembered Pamela's arrival at Camford House: her swift, confident stride, Bee's sudden tension. They looked utterly different now, linked by support and acceptance, yet nothing obvious occurred. Gillian only saw something tender in Bee's stance or the inclination of her head that she had never seen before. The tableau dissolved; the women moved behind the screen of leaves until, walking a little apart, they came into public view by the gate. Bee nodded to Gillian but did not speak.

After a minute or two, during which Gillian listened to the soft hum of an insect and contemplated the smooth-barked, muscular limbs of the beech tree, two large, black vehicles came slowly down the road and stopped directly in front of the gate. Denham emerged from one of them and opened the door for a tall, ungainly woman wearing an ancient black straw hat and a black dress on which traces of rust betrayed long disuse. The material whispered as she moved; moths might have flitted blindly from its folds. A sister, Gillian guessed, she's of the same generation.

The vicar went to meet them. He was as tall as Denham and not many years older; he might have been kin to the sister, but not, Gillian thought, to the brother, whose smooth white hand with its polished nails was at that moment grasping the vicar's brown, nodular fingers. The sister had Denham's blue eyes and a smaller edition of the family nose, but she was as weathered as an old fortress beneath the frayed brim of her hat. She moved decisively through the gate and stood stiffly while Denham slid into place beside her and the pallbearers prepared to remove the long, plain oak box from the other vehicle. Gillian watched them lift it.

The vicar then straightened his shoulders, swept them all with a glance in signal that he was ready and led the small procession towards the church.

'I am the resurrection and the life, saith the Lord: he that believeth in me, though he were dead, yet shall he live: and whosoever liveth and believeth in me shall never die.' The words comforted Gillian, although she did not believe, although she was sure Alistair Greenwood had believed no more than she. It was cold inside the church, but light, for the windows were of plain glass and the walls were whitewashed. Greenwood had doubtless passed many hours here; he had observed the orthodoxies of his world. 'For a thousand years in thy sight are but as yesterday: seeing that is past as a watch in the night.' The vicar had a strong, clear voice, and the words resonated through the vaulted, empty space. Tears escaped Gillian's eyes.

When the time came to leave the church, she saw to her surprise that Edward was there. He had entered noiselessly, and no one but the vicar had noticed his arrival. She could not turn and scrutinize the other faces, but she knew Edward was watching them all.

They filed past him through the door and across the dense, coarsebladed turf to the waiting grave. Gillian was disconcerted by the warmth of the day; she had forgotten it, inside. The mourners gathered, Edward lingering a little outside the group, and soon Greenwood's body was lowered into the grave and earth was strewn on the coffin. The vicar's calm voice reciting the Lord's Prayer anaesthetized Gillian's spirits, recalling a thousand moments of childhood: heads bent passively over small desks, voices more or less in unison murmuring a succession of half-comprehended syllables.

'Thy Kingdom come. Thy will be done…' She lost track of the words.

The ceremony came to its measured end, and the little knot of people began to unravel. Denham and his sister, dry-eyed and composed, talked with the vicar for several minutes. The others waited, saying little but wanting to take their leave properly—not wanting to hurry away as if this event had been sandwiched between others. Gillian was about to go and speak to Pamela and Bee when she found Smallbone at her elbow.

'It was good of you to come,' he said, sounding proprietary. Gillian was offended. 'I wanted to be here.'

'I drove from Norwich again. Fortunately my car gave me no trouble. After my problems with it on Monday, I was most reluctant to risk another trip, but I couldn't do otherwise, really. That lunch on Sunday—and then I'm an old student, and we'd kept up our friendship over the years—'

His phrases sounded rehearsed yet disjointed, and his eyes darted about, now watching Gillian, now scanning the other little groups. Gillian thought: You are not only a toad, you are a lying toad. You were no friend of Greenwood's; you are manufacturing a myth. She tried to edge away, but he kept talking.

'No one can take his place...such a shocking loss...Fiona Clay...it was all over the papers this morning. She was quite off her head, I thought. A drug addict, probably. And so frightfully melodramatic. Is that why she shot him at King's, d'you think?' His voice sank. 'What are people saying about it?'

Gillian looked at him with distaste. 'If you want information, why don't you ask him?' she said, indicating Edward, who was standing near enough to overhear them. 'He's a policeman.'

'Oh,' said Smallbone, absolutely disconcerted.

Gillian moved away to join Bee and Pamela, a few words were exchanged, Denham came over, more words—automatic—and then departure. The little assembly began to move in a straggling line towards the gate. Edward fell into step beside Gillian, a little behind the others.

'I didn't know you were coming,' she said.

'I wasn't certain. But in fact I was here before you. I saw you arrive.'

'Where were you?'

'Up there, behind those yew trees, in the MG. Racing green is relatively inconspicuous out here in all this bucolic profusion.'

'I never noticed you. I was too preoccupied.'

'So was everyone else. I see they all came except Toby. Where's he?'

'He decided not to cancel a lecture.'

'I see. A practical man.' They passed out of the gate and walked towards the Mini amid the noise of other vehicles backing and turning. 'I'm sorry,' Edward continued, 'I must be off straight away. Hardy's expecting me, and I may go down to London later. Will you be in tomorrow morning?'

'I can be.'

'Good. I may need you. I'll let you know, in any event.'

She got into the car, and he leaned on the door, his head at the open window.

'What d'you think, Gillian?'

'Not Fiona.'

'Why not?'

'Because Alistair Greenwood never laid eyes on her before Sunday, I'll swear it. There was no liaison. He wasn't hiding a discreditable private life; the point about Greenwood is that he had *no* private life.'

'Anything else?'

'If she had done it, she'd have killed him at his house.'

'I agree with you. And I hope that in a day or two we'll be able to talk of something else for a change.'

Gillian nodded. Her hand lay lightly on the steering-wheel, and he covered it with his own. 'Who called his wife "my gracious silence?" I can't remember, but I hope she very quietly kicked him in the arse.'

He was gone.

Edward drove slowly away from Little Camford, thinking of what he had seen. He had elected to arrive early, to sit in his car, observing and unobserved. The entrance to the churchyard did not lie upon the main road through the village, but gave on to a smaller road that curved away to the north past the church and an outlying cottage or two. Edward had parked beneath the trees near the corner of the churchyard, where the road bent. Only the vicar had been there before him.

Of the rest, Greenwood's housekeeper and her husband appeared first, walking arm in arm. Mrs. Hill wore a hat and gloves, and the pair went unhesitatingly through the gate, treading a familiar path. Probably does something for the church, Edward thought, maybe her husband keeps the grass trimmed.

Next came Victor Smallbone in his Morris. He drove up, parked on the grass verge some fifty feet short of the gate and sat there for a moment as though unsure that he had done the right thing. Then he stood by the car, peering over its roof at the churchyard to see who was there. He fidgeted. After a minute or two, Cecil Corbett, whom Edward did not know but whose face he remembered having seen in the Chetwynd Room, pulled in behind the Morris, and Smallbone pounced on him. Corbett looked faintly embarrassed. Doesn't care for Smallbone's company, Edward speculated, or possibly he already knows that the coveted Cambridge post will be offered to someone else.

They entered the gate, and the little road lay empty and silent. A few cars passed through the village. Then Gillian arrived in Bee's Mini. She barely glanced at the other vehicles; her eyes were fixed in the direction of the church. Edward, too, could see its square, compact tower, solid against the sky. Gillian disappeared through the gate. He waited.

The next car was Pamela's Jaguar, which, in contrast to the rumbling Mini, slid almost noiselessly into place just ahead of the Morris. Edward could see two people inside it, their heads bent close. Then they got out, Pamela on one side, Bee on the other. Pamela stood motionless, as if gathering her forces, and Bee came round the car to her. She never took her eyes from the other woman, and Edward, watching her face, thought: It's all she can do not to take her in her arms. Then, as they moved towards the gate, entering the field of vision of those within, they stepped deliberately apart and assumed a different air.

The implications of this little scene were superimposed on the images like subtitles in Edward's mind, and his thoughts were busy when the two black vehicles containing Greenwood's body and his family came to a dignified stop before the gate. He noted Denham's composure and correctly divined the identity of his female companion, but he saw nothing that added to his stock of information.

Once inside the church, he had been drawn into the occasion, into the tempo of the ceremony. He had let himself drift, snapping into watchfulness again only when the others were about to turn round and discover his presence.

In that brief instant, Edward's glance flickered swiftly from face to face, capturing surprise blended with other expressions: Victor's furtive embarrassment, Pamela's resentment, Bee's apprehension. Denham opened his eyes in ironical query; his sister paid no attention to Edward until Denham muttered something in her ear, whereupon she stared at Edward with a mixture of curiosity and disdain.

Alone in the car, he smiled to himself, thinking of the Rolls-Royce and the wine. He was still reviewing his data as he negotiated his way through Cambridge. The traffic was backed up along the edge of Parker's Piece, and he swore at the delay. He was eager to leave for London, but he could not go without seeing Hardy.

CHAPTER 17

Hardy was in his office, and the chain of paper-clips begun earlier that day now snaked across the desk and hung nearly to the floor. He looked up and said, 'I've got some tit-bits for you. I've been talking to Detective-Constable Petrie. He's found a student who knocked on Fox's door in college at four-thirty on Monday. Fox didn't answer.'

'Hmm. We can ask him where he was, but he'll stick to his story.'

'There's something else. Ditton didn't leave dinner at ten o'clock as she said; she was seen leaving before nine-thirty.'

'That's interesting. Did she lie or was she merely mistaken about the time? What difference could that half-hour make?'

'If she knew that Clay died between nine-thirty and ten…'

'It would have been safer not to lie, even then.'

'Name me a mistake more common among criminals than lying unnecessarily.' Hardy leaned back in his chair. He picked up the box of paper-clips and set it down again. It was empty. 'There's nothing on Smallbone yet,' he continued. 'According to him, when his car overheated he was on the A11, only a mile or two from Wymondham. I've got a man making inquiries there. So—what's your news? How was the funeral?'

'They were all there, except Fox, who was giving a lecture, I'm told. I ruffled a few feathers.'

'Smallbone came back from Norwich?'

'Yes. And he was so eager for information that he tried pumping Gillian Adams. It was clumsy and tasteless.'

'What did she tell him?'

'Nothing. She was rude to him instead. He's obviously a terrible gossip, but he was nervous, as well—ill at ease about being there.' Edward chatted on about Smallbone, conscious of a reluctance to tell Hardy about Bee and Pamela. What he had witnessed was hardly conclusive, and he was disgusted by rude official intrusion into the private lives of innocent persons. But perhaps they weren't innocent. If Greenwood had tried to blackmail Pamela into ending her affair, to force her hand by threatening to change his will....There had been more than a hint of menace in his attitude...he doubtless could have made Pamela's life in Cambridge a misery...what if Bee knew? It could all be relevant to the case. Or not.

While he was still talking about Smallbone, he decided to omit his guess about the two women. It could be brought in later, if necessary. Meanwhile, Hardy's thoughts had shifted direction. 'So Fox was the only one who didn't show up. I've been thinking about him. He had a good reason to want Greenwood to die before any damage was done. What if he killed Greenwood himself—and then pushed Clay into the river, making it look as if she'd done it?'

'That's quite possible. Let's hear the rest.'

'Now look. He could have gone to Little Camford Sunday night and taken the gun. Then he could have telephoned Clay and arranged to meet her—'

'How?'

'A threat. He told her he'd go to the police and tell them what had happened on Sunday if she didn't agree to meet him.' Hardy was getting excited. 'She goes back to Cambridge Monday evening; he shoots Greenwood, meets Clay later as arranged, she meanwhile having been swilling gin because she's frightened, he gives back the gun and then shoves her into the Cam. We find her the next day—or she disappears for a few days, which lures us into spending all our energy trying to find her—and when we do, she has the gun, and presto—Greenwood's murder is solved.'

Edward smiled. 'Excellent. It's a simpler construction than our previous attempt. But there is a problem: where was Clay while Fox shot Greenwood?'

Hardy did not look crestfallen. He grinned at Edward. 'That's a hole that can be patched.'

Edward laughed. 'All right. Let's suppose we have one murderer and two victims—Greenwood and Clay. Who fits the pattern?'

The case had reached a delicate point. Edward knew what line he wanted to pursue, but he wanted Hardy's cooperation. Even if the case were solved quickly, he would not consider that he'd done a satisfactory job if Hardy and others under him who had worked on the case were left with the feeling that he'd parachuted in and outwitted them all. And there was another problem. Edward's theory had one of Hardy's great bloody holes in it. 'X,' said Edward to himself, returning to old habits, 'had to know where Clay was at the time of Greenwood's death, to be certain she didn't have an alibi. She was stashed somewhere, probably with a few bottles. But where?'

Hardy said, 'Ditton fits, that's clear. And Bee Hamilton can be made to fit, if she was able to leave her house Sunday night without waking her husband.'

'She could probably have managed that. They're not sharing a bedroom.'

'And Smallbone—the schedule's tight, but it's possible. Any one of them could have met her by the river. And then there's Denham. He could have brought her from London, I suppose. Can we make that fit?'

'I think so,' said Edward. 'He could have driven up from London, leaving at three and arriving at King's before five. The traffic's dicey getting out of London at that hour, but once away, that car of his would eat up the miles.'

'The Lagonda? But it's too conspicuous.'

'He has a Mercedes, as well. A quiet grey one. So. He drives to Cambridge, puts a big hole in his little brother and then drives like hell back to London. He could have been back in St John's Wood by seven. It's a risk, but he knows we'll have to handle the panic here before we can think of telephoning London and sending someone round to inform him. Once he receives the news, his obvious duty is to come up here right away. He collects Clay, returns her gun, parks by the river and drops her in. Then he ambles along and presents himself at the station.'

'But how did he get the gun?' Hardy looked gloomy. 'I wish we could find some love-letters, or a sharp-eyed night clerk who'd seen Professor Greenwood and Clay off somewhere on a dirty weekend. It would be so much simpler. Where was Fiona Clay when Greenwood was shot? That's what we need to know.'

'Just so. But we have to keep working with the pieces we've got. There are two ends to this case, Cambridge and London. I'd like to spend a few hours in London today; I've a fancy to have a sniff at Denham's bailiwick. And I'd like you to handle the Cambridge end. See what you can find out about Fox—'

'Yes. I'd like to ask him where he was at four-thirty.'

'You can do that, but he won't budge. Whoever committed both murders is sharp-witted and has played a nicely calculated game. He's not likely to break under questioning. We'll have to hammer every nail if we're to lay charges. Fox is more breakable than the other two, but I don't like to use a crowbar on my suspects unless I'm forced to. It's a crude dirty tool, and, besides, there's always the chance that the confession won't stand up in court. I'm certain we can find the evidence we need if we keep looking. See what you can do about Fox and about Denham's car. Clay went into the river not a hundred yards from the car park by the wading pool in Lammas Land.'

'That's a lonely place at night, and anyone with a car would just have to lead her or carry her a little way over the grass.

The river is well screened there, too. On a misty evening, even the car would be barely visible from a short distance. I doubt we'll find anyone who saw it. But there's a house owned by St John's that's half way along the road to the car park. Maybe someone there heard a car pass, or saw one. I'll find out. If someone actually saw a Mercedes, or a Mini or—what does Ditton drive?'

'A tan Jaguar saloon.'

'Or a Jaguar, we'll be a long step further ahead.'

'Good luck to you, then.'

'Good hunting in London.'

Edward went back to his office and left a brief message for Jagger at the Yard. Ten minutes later he was driving south on the Trumpington Road in his battered MG, having noted the exact time of his departure. It wasn't really an accurate test, not the same car nor the same time of day, and he didn't even know which route Denham had taken, but he was interested in how long it would take him to reach St John's Wood.

The countryside unfurled before him: flat fields of ploughed earth, rows of unharvested cabbages and turnips, then low green hills and small towns of reddish-brown or mustard brick. He encountered little traffic until he reached the outskirts of London, but there the road became clogged. Nevertheless, he passed Denham's house one hour and twenty minutes after he had left the centre of Cambridge.

'Allow another five minutes for Denham to walk from King's to his car, and ten minutes for the press of traffic leaving Cambridge just before five-thirty,' Edward muttered to himself, 'and Denham would be snugly at home by five minutes to seven.'

He kept driving, creeping south towards Victoria Street. Driving through the centre of London seemed to become slower each day. The sky had clouded over, a fitful drizzle thickened the air, and London dripped, a grey and red water-colour like those sold on the pavement beside Green Park in kinder weather. The red buses throbbed patiently in the packed throng of cars. Edward was happy, drifting sluggishly past the infinite variety of façades and faces. London never grew stale.

Nearly half an hour later, he arrived in Victoria Street. New Scotland Yard, a blank behemoth set among the smaller, older buildings near the St James' Park tube stop, was unbeautiful, but acceptable because utterly familiar. Edward might have said the same about Jagger. Jagger was large— huge, to be accurate—with a face like a cement wall. He had small, unblinking, colourless eyes and a deceptive look of dull immobility. He could have enjoyed an interminable career playing hired thugs in the grade Bs, and in fact he had a furtive passion for crime stories and haunted the bookstalls in search of ones he hadn't read. Edward got on well with him; inside Jagger's bullet-shaped skull lurked an agile brain, one capable of surprising even old acquaintances. He knew his business thoroughly.

'You're not back?' he said when Edward strolled into his office.

'Of course not. I'm here for a little fishing.'

Jagger grunted. 'I've got something on your trout.'

'Good. What is it?'

'What the Americans would call his Dun and Bradstreet. Denham has a few quid to play with. It's not the kind of money you'd have heard about, not that much, but he can write a cheque for a million pounds—sometimes.'

'Sometimes?'

'His fortunes go up and down. He takes large risks— venture capital, they call it. At the moment, he's probably somewhat short of ready cash. He and some other gentlemen have just put up a large office block in the City, near the Barbican. Space there should sell; the Barbican is expected to have that effect, but at the moment the block is as quiet as a tomb. Empty. The interest must be totting up at quite a clip.'

'That's the way the money goes, Pop goes the weasel,' sang Edward softly. 'Splendid. Now, what else?'

'Nothing much. He's had quite a string of girlfriends, being the work-hard-play-hard type, I suppose. The house in St John's Wood is owned outright, a freehold he bought about five years ago. Before that, he had a flat overlooking Regent's Park. He went to Eton, two years ahead of his brother, who made his life a misery by outshining him in every conceivable way. He didn't endure that with grace, but then the young Alistair was constantly rubbing his nose in it.'

'What about university?'

'Never went. Never even applied, I'd guess. It was straight to the City and the money.'

'I imagine he couldn't face the prospect of Alistair's triumphal advance. I can't say I blame him. But it's curious that over the years he kept visiting his brother in Cambridge—like biting on a sore tooth.'

'What's curious about that?' Jagger said. 'He'd be after the money, wouldn't he? He's made his own pile, but he skates pretty near the edge now and then. He wouldn't want to lose sight of half a million quid if he thought he might inherit it.'

Edward shook his head. 'No. The money can't be the mainspring. He didn't take Fiona to Cambridge to ingratiate himself. I think he's spent his entire life trying to score off the arrogant Alistair and being snubbed for his pains. Not only by him, I should say,' he added, thinking of Toby's views on rich Americans and Pamela's phrase, 'a vulgar little man', which had come into Gillian's account of the ill-starred Sunday lunch.

'And the scabrous Miss Clay?'

'Jagger! You've been reading the dictionary again. Where will it all end?'

'It's these ruddy crime novels they write these days. More novel than crime—you need a dictionary and a B.Litt to understand 'em.'

'Write one,' said Edward. 'Bring back the gun and the blonde! Resurrect the monosyllable! But we were discussing Miss Clay—who doubtless never read a book in her life.

Denham took her to lunch—a case of *épater les* Cantabrigians, which she did—but with her own unpredictable flourishes. The gun, now—'

'I can tell you something more about that,' interrupted Jagger. 'We've squeezed one of our sources who knows Rex Green. It seems that Green has made himself scarce because he's in a spot of trouble with one of his playmates—a rough one. He's hardly been seen—apart from that quick dive into his bookmaker's. He disappeared suddenly, a couple of weeks ago, without collecting the gun or a large bundle of money he'd left at Fiona's flat. Fiona, being a girl who needs money, spent it. The word is that when he'd settled his differences with his disgruntled colleague, he was going to cut her up. And without that pretty face of hers, she'd have been finished.'

'I see. So she armed herself. What a wonderful world.'

Jagger shrugged. 'Well, what now? You didn't need to come to London to hear my newsy bits and pieces.'

'I wanted to poke about a bit. I wasn't certain where, but I am now. You and I, my friend, are going to pay a visit to Denham's empty office block.'

'With his key?'

'We'll find one of the other gentlemen. None of them should have reason to object, if we spin the right sort of tale.'

As they left the room, Jagger's telephone rang. It was Hardy. 'I've got some news for you. We've found a good citizen in Wymondham who saw Victor Smallbone's Morris spewing steam beside the road between six and half past Monday evening. He thinks he could identify Smallbone.'

'I'm relieved to hear it,' Edward replied. 'Scratch Smallbone.'

'And I just thought you'd like to know that a car was heard going down the road to the car park at about eleven o'clock Monday night. And it came back five or ten minutes later. One of the residents was out in the garden enjoying a late-night cigar. He didn't see the car, just the headlamps, but we're on the right track.'

'What did it sound like?'

'Quiet.'

'Ah. Good work. I'll be back this evening with news of my own, I hope.' Edward glanced out of the window and then followed Jagger. He wished he had brought his mackintosh. Now it was raining in earnest.

CHAPTER 18

Two hours later, Edward and Jagger were standing in the pitiless emptiness of the main entrance to the office block. Thirty storeys of vacant cubicles loomed above them.

'What do you expect to find?' Jagger asked.

'I expect nothing. He's had time to clean up. What I'd like to find is a bottle of gin, empty, and covered with fingerprints.'

'Not a hope.'

'But there may be something. Where the hell do we start?'

'At the top.'

'Right. He probably told her he wanted to show her the view.'

The thirtieth floor was not divided into offices. It was a vast, glass-walled flat surrounded by a staggering panorama of London. Off to the south, the vast, grey dome of St Paul's was visible through the rain. To the west, and far below them, lay Smithfield Market. 'Handy location,' observed Jagger. 'Not far from the Old Bailey.'

'Far enough, if we don't find what we're looking for. I wonder who will occupy this astounding flat.'

'Denham wouldn't have used it. There'd be a risk that one of his partners would bring someone here to admire the view.'

Edward groaned. 'I suppose you're right. That means searching the bloody offices. How many of them are there?'

'Too many. We'll have to narrow the field. I still say start at the top, but not this floor or the next one down. These new buildings are always too cheap to be well sound-proofed. Let's try twenty-eight and then twenty-seven.'

'Lead on. I'll follow like an Arab wife.'

They went down the stairs, Jagger manoeuvring his heavy bulk with purposeful speed, Edward quick and light-footed behind. 'By the way, why did you say *sayonara?* You promised I'd find out when I got back.'

'How's your karate?' said Jagger over his shoulder.

'My karate? I'm not on *The Sweeney*. I just hit people. If I have to.'

'Your primitive methods are out of favour. The Assistant Commissioner has a new idea.'

'Oh no.'

'Oh yes. You may think it's enough to bang your villain against brick walls, but now you must learn to kick him in the chin.'

Edward raised his fists to heaven. 'Oh bugger it all!'

The twenty-eighth floor consisted of a large central open space with a vast window looking north, a frieze of offices around the perimeter and a number of smaller, central cubicles without windows. The rooms were all locked, and even with a master key it was a tedious job to open each one. The glassy, carpeted boxes varied slightly in size, but their sameness in all other respects deadened the senses. It was difficult after a short time not to close each door after one cursory, dull-eyed glance within. A search of the entire floor yielded nothing. The two men looked at each other. 'Twenty-seven.' They went down another flight of stairs and began again.

Twenty-seven was divided into smaller boxes, and its future receptionist would command fewer acres of window and carpet. They went their dreary way along the rim and then turned to the inner rooms. There was nothing.

'Now what?' said Edward.

'Twenty-six,' Jagger replied doggedly. He started for the stairs.

'Wait! Jagger, we're a pair of idiots. If Denham locked her in this building for twenty-four hours with some bottles of gin, he damned well wouldn't choose a room with a carpet. All we need to do is look in the lavatories on each floor.'

On the twentieth floor, they found it. As they opened the door marked Ladies, a faint but recognizable odour of vomit and disinfectant wafted past them. They saw a small, tiled space containing two basins set into a formica counter, a rectangular looking-glass, and, beyond, two cubicles. The room had been swabbed, and had the door not been closed, the smell would no longer have been noticeable. There were no bottles.

'We'll have to have every inch checked for prints. He may have missed one.' They stood just in the doorway, not moving, not wanting to obliterate the minuscule traces that might lie invisible on the floor. But their eyes travelled inexorably over each surface, fiercely inspecting every tiny irregularity.

'Go downstairs and ring the Yard. See whether we can get a squad right away. I'll stay here. Denham may have got wind of us by now, and I'm not giving him a second chance to mop up.' Jagger went. Edward remained in the doorway, looking. He could no longer smell anything.

Ten minutes later, Jagger was back. 'They'll be round in half an hour.'

Edward hadn't moved. He pointed to the wall beneath the basins. 'Look at the far corner where the tile meets the painted wall. Can you see anything there?'

Jagger stared, puckering his eyelids in a porcine squint. 'A hair?'

'A black hair.'

'That'll be enough for the lab.'

'It will prove she was here, but not exactly when. I'll be content when I can either connect Denham to the gun or prove he was in Cambridge at five-twenty on Monday. Preferably both.'

In the evening, Edward drove back to Cambridge, where he found Hardy waiting for him with unconcealed impatience and an air of saturnine glee.

'I detect a whiff of triumph,' said Edward. 'Shall I tell you first, or will you tell me? "For there is good news yet to hear and fine things to be seen. Before we go to Paradise by way of Kensal Green."'

Hardy took no notice of Edward's lapse into frivolity. He set himself to tell a story. '"Look for the car," you said. So off I went and looked for the bloody car. And the first thing I found was what I told you this morning: that an unidentified car had been seen on the road to the Lammas Land car park. But I couldn't get any further with that, so I tried a different line. I knew there was no point in trying to find where the Mini and the Jaguar were at five-fifteen; Ditton and Fox live here, and their cars probably stayed put all day. But if Denham was here at five-fifteen, he must have parked somewhere near King's. Otherwise, he'd be cutting his time too fine. Lion Yard's the obvious place, and I was sure that if he'd parked there, we'd never get a sniff of the car. Hundreds of vehicles go in and out all day. But I didn't think he would park there because he'd have had to pay the attendant and risk being remembered. I sent Petrie along anyhow, to see the attendants who were on duty Monday afternoon. Nothing. And I knew he wouldn't have parked illegally: a ticket would have been fatal.'

Hardy was spinning out his tale, enjoying the taste of it. 'What choices did he have, then? Queen's Road, Silver Street, Botolph Lane. But what do you think I discovered next?' He paused expectantly.

'I've no idea. To the uninitiated, the mysteries of Cambridge parking are unfathomable.'

'There was a concert at King's College Chapel that afternoon,' Hardy announced triumphantly. Everyone who can goes to those. Denham Greenwood wouldn't have found a place to park anywhere near King's, not to save his life. And that left only one possibility: the college car parks.'

'Ah.'

'I checked those myself. Not King's, I thought. Too conspicuous. I went to Pembroke instead. Have you seen their car park? It's a small, dark, handy little space just off Pembroke Street. Perfect for Denham. They have a hell of a time with illegal parking, being so near the market. They used to have one of those confounded poles that you unlock with a special key, but some bright lad drove over it backwards and broke it. Anyhow, I popped in and had a word at the porter's lodge about who might have noticed an outlaw Mercedes in the car-park on Monday afternoon. And they put me on to Ivor Fleming. He's one of the Fellows, and he has a bee in his bonnet about unauthorized parking. Complains regularly and bitterly to the porters about it. They said he'd have noticed the Mercedes if anyone had. So I called on him. His rooms overlook Pembroke Street; damned cold in winter, I shouldn't wonder. Fleming's an eccentric sort of bird, a chemist. He's in college every day, but he lives out, just over in Botolph Lane, and he leaves his car in Pembroke. He has a mania for orderly detail—maybe all chemists are like that. Well, he was very cordial and polite, and when I told him I'd come about a Mercedes that had no business to be where it was, he was pleased as punch. He went on about that bleeding car park for five minutes before I could get a word in. Eventually, though, I asked him about Monday, and it took him only a few seconds to work it out. He'd nipped home, through the car park, at about a quarter past five, as usual, and there was a big grey Mercedes parked right next to his old Austin. He was going to mention it to the porters and ask whether it belonged to a guest, but by the time he went back, the car was gone. That was at about six o'clock. He didn't remember the number, just that there were two eights, but he did know the year: it was W. That's nineteen-eighty-one, and it's the right one.'

Hardy smiled ferociously. 'I think we've got him.'

'Yes, I do believe we have.' Edward briefly related what he had been doing in London. 'The hair is on its way to

Nottingham, where it will be matched to the ones on Clay's head.'

Hardy's chain of paper-clips was lying forgotten on the floor beside his desk. He leaned over and picked it up, whirling it about his head. Edward leaned back in his chair and crossed his ankles, pleased with the world and the day's work.

'But you know,' said Hardy, letting the chain go so that it sailed off into a corner, 'I was surprised. I thought that if Fiona hadn't done it on her own, Fox would be our man. And how did Denham steal the gun in time? He was in London Sunday night.'

'That's precisely what I want to clear up next. I'm going back to Camford House tomorrow, when it's light.'

The next morning, Edward telephoned Gillian and arranged to pick her up at Bee's house. During the night, the clouds had dispersed, and it was another cool, fair autumn day.

'Well?' she said as she slid into the MG.

'It's tied up—except one loose thread. We're going back to Camford House now to see what can be done about it. I don't want some needle-witted defence counsel to pull on it and unravel my case.'

Gillian waited, not daring to ask the question. Edward's eyes were on the traffic, but she saw the corner of his mouth lift in a smile.

'What admirable restraint,' he remarked. He let several seconds go by and then added, 'It shall be rewarded. The answer to the question you are burning to ask is this: I'm going to London this afternoon to arrest Denham Greenwood.'

'Really?' squeaked Gillian. 'I thought he probably—but I wasn't ever sure. God, it seems so quick now, and yet the last few days have been interminable.'

'You suspected him, then. Why?'

'An intuitive process, I guess. Because Greenwood was killed at King's. Who else would have done that? Toby, possibly; he has a grudge against King's. But he wouldn't have wanted to make such a mess. And none of the others would have desecrated the holy ground. But I wasn't sure—I had my own prejudices to contend with.'

A constable was still on duty at Camford House, but not the same one, for which Gillian was grateful. In the garden the chestnut trees, still green only a few days earlier, were a brilliant gold. They entered the house for the last time. The morning light shone through the windows, but the rooms seemed sombre, as empty as on Monday evening and more deeply wrapped in stillness. Mrs. Hill had not been back, and a faint film of dust was already beginning to settle.

'What do you want me to do?' asked Gillian as Edward led the way to the dining-room.

'I want you to think about where everyone was from the moment you all left the dinning-room. Just suppose, my love, that while you were buried in Gibbon and Greenwood was chauffeuring the prostrate Mrs. Hill, that somebody toddled quietly into the dining-room and rifled the sideboard.'

Gillian's eyes widened. 'Of course. It's quite possible. But it can't have been Denham—he'd left.'

'Had he? There was a row with Fiona in the car, he said. Or she could have passed out again. He knew his brother was planning to take Mrs. Hill home. If he idled in the lane, he would have seen the Rolls leave. He could easily have returned to the house, with an excuse ready, if he were seen.'

'OK. Let me think. Denham and Fiona left the house. Greenwood shoved us summarily into the garden, went back in and brought coffee a few minutes later. Did you ever find the bullet that had been taken from the wall?'

'The scenes of crime squad found it in the rubbish bin.'

'So Greenwood probably did dig out the offending object. Well, Mrs. Hill must have been cleaning the dining-room while we had coffee, because it was tidy when I went in after I left the library. After a few minutes, Greenwood took me into the library, and then he drove Mrs. Hill home. Pamela left then, too, going through the house just ahead of us. Wouldn't she or Greenwood have seen Denham's car?'

'Not if he waited in the lane past the bend in the opposite direction from the village.'

'All right. Let me get on with this before I become confused. I was in the library; Bee was busy being sick in the downstairs bathroom. Toby and Victor never came into the house. If no one is lying—and why should they if you're right—Denham probably had a clear ten minutes to get in and out of the house. He had to avoid Victor, who was nosing about behind the old stables.'

'If he walked straight through the trees, he would have been screened from the house and the stables all the way to the garage. He could have done it easily. And he needed no time at all inside. He knew how to open the drawer, or he wouldn't have tried it.'

'What about Fiona?'

'That's simple. Either she was unconscious, or he told her that he was going back for the gun and then pretended he'd failed. I expect she thought that's why they were returning to Cambridge Monday night: to try again. Let's look at that sideboard. There must be an easy way to open that drawer.'

'Not with the key. Greenwood had it in his pocket, and I refuse to believe that Denham carried a duplicate key about with him.'

Edward pulled an envelope from his pocket and shook out the other two keys. He jiggled first one and then the other in the lock of the centre drawer without success. Then he opened the other drawers, above and below, and stared irritably at the contents.

'Why did he lock up the teaspoons, I wonder?' Gillian sat beside him on the carpet.

'Old habits, probably. When the servants nick the silver, the teaspoons always go first.' He pulled the top drawer out a little further and shone his torch into the shadowy recess. There was nothing to see. He began to close the drawer again, but Gillian said 'Wait!' and put her hand over his. She pulled gently and steadily, and the long drawer slid outwards until it suddenly fell out and almost dropped into Edward's lap. Gillian caught it with her other hand. A dark, rectangular hole gaped where it had been. Edward lifted the torch and squinted downward into the recess. Gillian looked over his shoulder. What they could see was the empty inside of the middle drawer.

'There,' said Gillian triumphantly.

Edward looked amused. 'How simple. Too simple for a smart detective like me. How did you happen to think of it?'

'It was the spoons. I once dropped a whole drawerful of silver on my toe because it had no backstop, or whatever you call it, and I pulled it out too far.'

'You did. Hmph. Feminine intuition.'

'Rubbish. That's called experience. Your trouble is that you don't lead a full enough life. Pain leads to growth and understanding.'

'Your brains may be in your toes, mine aren't.'

'I will not laugh. I'm not about to have another young constable coming in here and looking censorious.'

Edward stood up and replaced the keys in the envelope, putting it and his small torch back in his pocket. 'That's that. I've got to go back to the station. As soon as the two reports I'm waiting for come through, I'm off to London.'

'Edward, what made you decide it was Denham?'

'I started where you did: King's. Someone wanted to make a point. When I couldn't find any connection between Clay and Greenwood, and I realized she was too incompetent to have stage-managed that episode, I began to think about who might have used her. Denham was the most plausible suspect.'

'Because he knew her.'

'Yes, and he had driven her back to London. But I did consider the other possibilities, particularly Toby and Pamela—and even Bee, because she's in love with Pamela.'

'How did you find that out?'

'I saw them together outside the churchyard. You knew about them?'

'Bee told me yesterday. But they've kept it quiet because Pamela didn't want anyone to know.'

'I fancy the "anyone" was Alistair Greenwood.'

'Well, anyone, but him particularly. Anyway, Bee wouldn't have told me about it if she had been mixed up with Greenwood's murder, or thought Pamela was. She told me last night that Pamela sneaked out of the back door Monday evening when I arrived, because she didn't want anyone to know she'd been there.'

'So that's where she was between nine-thirty and ten. People's little personal secrets are always gumming up the works. Anyhow, she and Bee didn't divert me for long. Denham seemed a much likelier candidate. Who else would have desired a scandalous death for Greenwood?'

'And to splatter Cambridge with blood while he was at it.'

They left the dining-room. 'Where will I find you this afternoon?' asked Edward.

'In Heffer's. I'm planning to spend all afternoon in the bookshops.'

'Is it anything like Foyle's? I'll never find you.'

'It's not. Foyle's gives me indigestion. Heffer's will only take all my money.'

'Never mind. I'll buy you a hamburger.'

'Not in Cambridge, you won't. They *boil* hamburgers here.'

'Never mind. I hope we'll be in London tonight.'

CHAPTER 19

Edward spent most of that day in his car. He returned to the station, where Hardy was waiting for him with the confirmation of Nottingham that the hair was one of Fiona Clay's. 'Then let's start for London,' said Edward. 'I don't know how long it will take to turn up all the relevant licence plates, but there can't be many nineteen-eighty-one grey Mercedes cars carrying plates with two eights.'

They roared down the M11; Edward was taking Hardy to London so he could be in at the kill. First, they collected Jagger at the Yard. The three of them then went to the City, where they made a neat and comradely job of arresting Denham Greenwood for the murders of Alistair Greenwood and Fiona Clay.

He received them calmly; they saw that he had been expecting them.

'Well, gentlemen, what can I do for you?'

They went through the formula.

'I'm afraid you have made an extremely costly error,' Denham responded coldly. 'But I have no doubt that it will be rectified. Sir Hugh Lyttleton—' he pronounced the name of the best and most expensive criminal lawyer in London— 'happens to be a friend of mine.'

'You'll need him,' said Jagger, and they escorted him out of the office, past the wondering and avid eyes of several secretaries.

In the afternoon, Edward left him in Jagger's capable hands and drove Hardy back to Cambridge. He bid an unregretful farewell to his little room overlooking Parker's Piece, and then he went to look for Gillian. He found her in front of the modern poetry section in Heffer's. Books—the uppermost being a copy of Greenwood's *Ruling Ideas*—were piled on the floor at her feet, and she was leafing through a collection of English verse. She did not notice him until he touched her shoulder.

'I was looking for this,' she said. 'Listen.'
' "I only know that you may lie
Day-long and watch the Cambridge sky,
And, flower-lulled in sleepy grass,
Hear the cool lapse of hours pass,
Until the centuries blend and blur…" '

'He may have been writing about Grantchester, but for me it's Cambridge too. It still is, despite what's happened. I walked along the Backs this afternoon, and past the Fellows' Garden at Clare, under the old lime trees and the stupendous copper beech near the river, and there was the small, stately court, a sort of perfect kernel, with the spires of King's hovering over it—like a guardian angel, as a lovely man I knew once said to me…and I could feel Greenwood's death slipping away, a little eddy in the tide of years. The centuries blend and blur. Poor Denham. He wanted to unravel the whole tapestry by pulling out a single thread—and he never even touched the fabric. Do you know what I mean?'

'I do, yes. But I've never felt the pull—either way. Even now. But then I've hardly seen Cambridge.'

'No, you haven't seen much of it, more's the pity. And there isn't the time now.' Gillian paused. 'I know. Come with me and I'll show you. We'll climb Great St Mary's together.' She shut the book and carried it to the counter with the others. Then she handed it, along with the copy of *Ruling Ideas*, to Edward. 'Here. These are for you. I'm glad we've been in Cambridge together, in spite of all. And these books

have the merit, among others, of being much shorter than
The Decline and Fall of the Roman Empire.'

'Yes, I can see that. Thank you,' said Edward gravely. They
linked arms and went out into the blue October afternoon.

'What will happen to Toby?'

Edward shrugged. 'So far as the police are concerned,
nothing. That's a university matter.'

'You talked to Cooper-Hewson about the *aegrotat.* I
wonder what he'll do.'

'That was in connection with Greenwood's death. Now
that the murder has been solved, he may forget about it.'

'And if he doesn't?'

'He'll find no evidence. Only a suggestive chain of cir-
cumstance. If Fox keeps his mouth shut, he can be convicted
of nothing but a piece of poor judgment.'

'In recommending a pass for a doubtful student.'

'Exactly.'

Trinity Street was in shadow, cut off from the westering
sun by the high walls of Caius. But at the bottom of the
street, Gillian and Edward emerged into sunshine in the open
space between King's College Chapel and Great St Mary's.
Cars and bicycles and pedestrians swirled around them as
they made their way across it and towards the entrance of
the church.

The door stood open. Inside, it was immediately dim and
cool and silent. A white-haired man sat patiently by a counter
full of postcards and pamphlets; he smiled gently but did
not speak except to thank them as they paid the entrance fee
for the tower. Past the counter, in the western wall of the
church, was a low, arched doorway and a crepuscular glimpse
of winding stair. Gillian went in and began to climb, Edward
following. The stone steps were steep and narrow and uneven,
worn by many feet, spiralling upward in the dim glow of a
few bare light bulbs. Occasional shafts of daylight, lancing
through slits in the tower wall, pierced the gloom. They
passed a small, locked door, and above that an opening

through which they could see the heavy ropes of the church bells passing through holes in a rough wooden floor. Then they came to the bells themselves, their great mouths titled upwards, enormous and silent.

The climb was long enough to accustom their eyes to the darkness, and when they suddenly stepped out into the full, level blaze of the late afternoon sunshine, they were momentarily too dazzled to see. No one else was there. The tower was high and square, with a heavy parapet and four pinnacles at the corners. Between these, strong wire mesh guarded the space above the parapet. There were square openings to afford unobstructed views; these were large enough for a head but too small for a body to pass through. In the centre was a raised platform bearing a display of faded, cloudy photographs of the panorama before them, with keys for identifying buildings of interest.

Gillian led Edward first to the eastern side, and they gazed down at the Market Square directly below, still full of life, though a few of the stalls were empty and others were getting ready to close. Cut flowers made brilliant patches of colour here and there among the weathered awnings and grey cobblestones; fragments of cheerful clatter drifted upwards through the autumn air. Beyond lay a dense, irregular mix of town buildings, ordinary and indistinguishable from this height and angle.

Next, they looked south, at the city again, at a long vista of small, low buildings in shades of grey, relieved only by the vast, pillared front of the Fitzwilliam Museum and the spire of the Catholic church. In the distance, the peaceful fields of Cambridgeshire made a horizon as flat as the sea.

Gillian said nothing but took Edward from the south to the north side, where the scene was dramatically different. In dizzying, steep perspective, the high, dormered, Victorian façade of Caius rose to meet them. Beyond it stretched a complex, intersecting array of college walls and geometrical glimpses of clipped green court, the Wren Library and, rearing up behind, bifurcating the horizon, the big, square tower of St John's Chapel with its narrow arched windows and four sharp pinnacles. The tightly clustered roof-planes and chimneys of the town huddled far below.

Having looked their fill, Gillian and Edward wandered at last to the western side of the tower and looked out at a spectacular sight. A sumptuous glitter of gold and green lay before them: just below, the perfect green rectangle of turf before the Senate House and the Old Schools, looking as smooth as a billiard table from so far above, and, on the left, King's College—the golden tracery of the gateway and screen set against the green velvet lawn of the court, and, further away, beyond the classical immensity of Gibbs' Building, the emerald sweep of the Backs and the silver ribbon of the Cam. In the midst of this setting, vast, glorious, golden, filling the sky, rose the chapel, its turrets and pinnacles catching the light of the descending sun.

Gillian and Edward drew breath and exclaimed like travellers unused to the world's surprises. Then they gazed silently, shading their eyes. At last, Gillian said, 'Well, there it is. As potent an image of perfection as you will ever see. And it's not simple to live in its shadow.'

Edward turned towards her. 'And what about you? Would you live here? Is that what you want?'

Gillian stared into the distance, where the moisture in the air turned the sky a silvery blue. 'I've wondered about that off and on for the last fifteen years. But now that I've come back at last, I know the answer. I'm not Cambridge material, as Greenwood might have—doubtless would have—said. In fact, it was Greenwood who convinced me. Not his death, but his life. The arsenic in the footnotes, as Steiner said. I'm afraid of being seduced by the past.'

Edward sighed. 'And I'm afraid of being seduced by you.'

'Why?'

'I'm off balance,' he said almost angrily.

'So am I. But isn't it better than not moving?'

'I don't know. Life at Madame Tussaud's was comfortable.'

She turned to look at him. 'What do you mean: "life"? How can you claim to be alive if you don't feel?'

'I did. I do. I love my work. I have friends. I'm pleased by books and sunsets and cool beer on a warm afternoon.'

'Books and sunsets and wine with dinner. Yes, I know what they are.'

'Well, then. A sunset never hurt anyone.'

'No. But I wouldn't say the same about books. Maybe you should stop reading, too.'

'Dammit, you're relentless.'

'I've got as much at stake as you have, you know.'

Edward smiled a little. 'And you're still reading?'

'It's what the book trade calls a page-turner.'

'Full of sex and violence? I'd feel safer in something by Henry James.'

'What do you think we are? A pair of Harold Robbins characters? Any more Jamesian restraint and we'd kick the effing bucket.'

Edward burst out laughing. 'Oh God! Christ,' he said and laughed some more.

She waited and then said, 'I don't know exactly why it is, but seeing you here has helped make things clear to me. You're a counterweight, somehow. You drag me into the present. You're concrete. And I need the city, not the cloister.'

'Then let's go back together. We'll have dinner somewhere and walk along the Embankment afterwards.' He gave her a look of wry affection. 'Come on. Tonight I'll show you the real London.'

Gillian smiled back, suddenly light of heart. Edward led the way down the dark, precipitous stair and out of the church towards the Market Square. They did not stop, but Gillian looked back over her shoulder at King's. The light was fading. Across the broad strip of turf and the cobbled street lay the gigantic, elongated shadow of the chapel.